Also by David Slavitt

FICTION

The Hussar *1987*
The Agent, *with Bill Adler 1986*
Alice at 80 *1984*
Ringer *1982*
Cold Comfort *1980*
Jo Stern *1978*
King of Hearts *1976*
The Killing of the King *1974*
The Outer Mongolian *1973*
ABCD *1972*
Anagrams *1970*
Feel Free *1968*
Rochelle, or Virtue Rewarded *1967*

NONFICTION

Physicians Observed *1987*
Understanding Social Psychology,
with P. Secord and C. Backman, 1976

POETRY

Equinox *1988*
The Tristia of Ovid *1986*
The Walls of Thebes *1986*
The Elegies to Delia of Albius Tibullus *1985*
Big Nose *1983*
Dozens *1981*
Rounding the Horn *1978*
Vital Signs: New and Selected Poems *1975*
The Eclogues and the Georgics of Virgil *1972*
Child's Play *1972*
The Eclogues of Virgil *1971*
Day Sailing *1968*
The Carnivore *1965*
Suits for the Dead *1961*

Salazar Blinks

◆

Salazar Blinks

❖ ❖ ❖ ❖ ❖ ❖ ❖ ❖ ❖ ❖

DAVID R. SLAVITT

COLLIER BOOKS
Macmillan Publishing Company
New York

Collier Books
Macmillan Publishing Company
866 Third Avenue, New York, NY 10022
Collier Macmillan Canada, Inc.

Library of Congress Cataloging-in-Publication Data

Slavitt, David R., 1935–
Salazar blinks / David R. Slavitt. — 1st Collier Books ed.
        p.   cm.
        ISBN 0-02-045211-X
    1. Salazar, António de Oliveira, 1889–1970—Fiction.
    2. Portugal—History—1910–1974—Fiction.   I. Title.
        PS3569.L3S35   1990
        813'.54—dc20   89-25168   CIP

Cover illustration © by Gary Kelly

First Collier Books Edition 1990

10   9   8   7   6   5   4   3   2   1

Printed in the United States of America

FOR MICHAEL CARLISLE,
OBRIGADO.

In this cursed country, all that is noble commits suicide;
all that is vulgar triumphs.
—MIGUEL DE UNAMUNO

◆

Portugal is not a joke country!
—GENERAL PIMIENTO DE SAMPAYO

◆

Acknowledgments

◆

The author wishes to acknowledge his reliance for many of the historical details of this novel upon Hugh Kay's excellent *Salazar and Modern Portugal* (Hawthorn Books, New York, 1970). The passages from Camões' *Os Lusiadas* are in the translation of William C. Atkinson, published by Penguin Books in 1952.

I

Salazar Blinks

◆

1

HE LIES THERE. *Hic jacet,* for indeed he looks like one of those figures carved in marble on a catafalque. Or his face does. An observer might, if he were of a certain disposition, take note of the tubing visible below, the catheters that drain away bodily wastes.

But even to advert to such matters is to approach satire, which is by no means my intention. How well I am aware of the plight of poor Diogo Bernardes (ca. 1530–1605?), who was chosen to write an epic on King Sebastian's Alcácer-Kebir expedition of 1578.

The expedition turned out badly.

Disastrously, in fact. The king led some 15,000 foot and 1,500 horse, and had 9,000 camp followers of every kind. There were 500 vessels. A mighty host in a mighty armada! And what happened to them? Eight thousand were killed, and 15,000 more were taken as slaves. Perhaps a hundred men survived and made it to the coast and eventual freedom. This is not the only century of folly and mass butchery. Those traditions are venerable.

Diogo nevertheless persevered, doing what he had contracted to do, for which honesty and good faith he was—of course—imprisoned. He wrote, thereafter, only religious poetry and bucolic verses full of love for nature and vivid descriptions of the Lima River.

A sad story?

Sobering, surely. For the Portuguese genius is for the epic. Not only Camões's *Os Lusiadas*, which is the only poem of our country known throughout Europe, but *Camões*, the epic on the neglect of genius by João Batista da Silva Leitao de Almeida Garrett.

Almeida Garrett is often called the Goethe of Portuguese literature. (Goethe is hardly ever called the Almeida Garrett of Germany.)

Is it better to attempt epics and fail or to be satisfied with trivialities and improvisations, and a life of *piadas* (anecdotes) and dissipation?

My destiny—and I do not think it an exaggeration to refer in that way to this translation from prison—is here, bound up with that unmoving body, inexpressive, but still alive.

Perhaps, as they insist, sentient?

Depending upon my mood, I hope he is sentient. Or fear he may be. The poet's relation to his audience is never what you'd call secure.

The doctors say Salazar cannot possibly recover. And yet they attend him, hoping, like me, in contrary directions.

António Vieira wrote: "God gave the Portuguese a small country as cradle but all the world as their grave." Typical in its gloomy pride, and now, three hundred years later, we are in similar circumstances. The quivering of the lips, the fluttering of the eyelids, the occasional catching of his labored breath may mean nothing at all; but it is difficult to resist thinking of these as the external signs of his dreams, the outward manifestations of an inner activity we can only guess at.

But what has Portugal been for the past forty years but the external manifestation of this man's dream life?

That I am his eyes and ears is my reward and my punishment. Life is more comfortable here than in jail. And yet my freedom is even more tightly circumscribed. They watch me and listen to me, of course.

I was flattered by my imprisonment. For a poet to be incarcerated is a kind of honor. It is a form of participation in the great tradition of Portuguese letters. Like Camões, I too was a student at Coimbra, and like him I have served time in a prison cell.

But it is also flattering for a poet to be attended, as I am now, by men of power and authority. Even by men who used to hold power—for this is no longer the actual government of the country.

Was it ever, I wonder? Were they ever of any more independent will than the implements on Salazar's desk?

In any event, Salazar's old cabinet is assembled here in the bedroom three mornings a week, and they pretend to meet and discuss the government of the nation. Or, no, they do actually meet and do in fact discuss the government. What they are pretending is that they still decide policy, that they determine what should be done about this and that, for whom and to whom.

Because there is no one bold enough, or crude enough, to inform the old man that he no longer governs.

How could he possibly dream that Caetano is now Prime Minister?

Unless I were to let him know, that is.

And what would my punishment be? Which of these old men still has even the authority to dispose of so unimportant a question as the proper penalty for the disobedience of the poet/journalist he was unwise enough to have approved in the first place?

I probably ought to set down the reason for my having been incarcerated. What harm can it do, after all? The mere existence of this document will be sufficient to put me away, in a cell, a torture chamber, or a shallow grave, depending upon the mood of the PIDE that day. Which is what happened last time, more or less.

I referred to "crocodile tears" in one of my poems, and that was interpreted—accurately, I must confess—as a reference to Angola and the troubles there.

But for a man like me not to write is to be unmanned, is a denial of so fundamental a piece of him as to disestablish his very existence.

Which is what they were trying to do—the PIDE and Dr. Salazar.

If there were a God, however slow and inefficient, whimsical and unreliable but yet fundamentally equitable and just, he would be tormenting Salazar as the PIDE has tormented so many thousands over these past forty years. These twitches and starts, these catches of breath and occasional gasps, would be the expression of . . . of such remorse. Of such pity for the cries of victims that sound in his large and rather hairy ears.

It is said that in Angola the ignorant were spared but the blacks with books, the ones who had believed what we'd told them, who had been taken in by our professions of superiority and who wanted to better themselves—they were the ones the PIDE or the army shot. Shot them and threw their children to the crocodiles. Or threw their children to the crocodiles first.

Then the bullet, which was, at that point, a mercy.

And it all came from this man's mind.

"Parliamentary democracy," he wrote, "has resulted in instability and disorder, or, what is worse, it has become a despotic domination by political parties. When matters come to a climax, dictatorships are created . . . so that a new beginning can be made."

And it's true enough. Liberalism deprives the people of the liberties it is supposed to safeguard.

And anyone who has read his Plato knows that the benevolent dictatorship of the philosopher kings is the ideal form of government for the republic. Or, as his government has been called, "the dictatorship of the professors."

Let us put it another way, more modestly but also more clearly. It has occurred to me that my destiny is now entwined with that of Dr. Salazar—and his condition is not exactly robust. When he dies, there will be a temptation to do away with certain kinds of detritus that remain behind the great

man. There is likely to be a cleaning up of his personal effects—
his collection of pornography, for instance, or the whips and
chains that he used in his younger days as aids to his libido.

No, there probably are not such items—poor man. He would
not have permitted himself such indulgences.

But my existence, this encounter of ours at least, would be
every bit as embarrassing to the monumental image his succes-
sors would want to preserve. I don't have to be very clever (or
very paranoid) to imagine the possibility (or is it a likelihood?)
that I may be killed the moment he expires.

Men have been killed for far less in this generation-long regime.

That he lay there, unable to move, unable to speak, merely
listening and, on occasion, blinking to make his will known to
his old associates, once for *yes*, twice for *no* . . . that's bad
enough.

Worse is the tawdry fact that he is indulged this way because
no one in Portugal is man enough to tell him the truth, to
confront him, braving the twitches and gasps, and say loudly
enough and slowly enough for a stone to understand, "Dr.
Salazar, you are no longer governing our country. Portugal has
new rulers."

Some country he has left behind him!

I am his last subject.

The rest of the country obeys Caetano—as I do, too, I
suppose. But when Salazar blinks, and a new rule is promul-
gated or a new policy approved in the fantasy government of
which he remains in control, there must be some consequence,
some tangible result, mustn't there?

Some mention, at the very least, in the newspapers and on
the radio?

He cannot read a newspaper. But he can hear a radio program on which I am the reporter and newscaster, reading the
dispatches my masters have approved and adding to them new
ones they have instructed me to write.

He may or may not hear them.

If he hears them, he may or may not believe them. After
all, he knows what it is like to have the press controlled by the
government. Bad news never gets printed or broadcast.

Still, it's better here than in jail. The food is better and I can walk in the walled garden. My life is not exactly free and expansive . . . but neither was his before the stroke.

If I were to complete this manuscript, or even to write a substantial piece of it and somehow smuggle it out, then everything would be different. Then they couldn't kill me! The only way to insure my silence would be to keep me alive.

Of course, if they catch me with it before I manage to smuggle it out, I shall be in something of a difficulty.

One cannot figure the odds too closely. It is my nature to write. I am a writer. I ought to write.

2

YES, YES, THERE IS A GARDEN. There is a bedroom. There is a studio where I read my dispatches into a microphone that is attached to the speaker in the radio by Salazar's bed (and to other speakers as well, I must suppose, in the offices of those who supervise this peculiar operation).

But I cannot say for certain where I am. In Lisbon, I presume. I assume that they've moved me from the Aljube, which is the PIDE prison, to Salazar's residence, but they might just as well have moved Salazar to some obscure place of internment to which they brought me, too.

I have glimpsed the famous Dona Maria, who has been Salazar's housekeeper since his student days at Coimbra—or a woman who looks like her.

An extraordinary story, that. António de Oliveira Salazar and Manuel Gonçalves Cerejeira sharing their digs at Coimbra, and the one becomes Portugal's temporal ruler while the other rises in the church until he is the Cardinal Patriarch of Lisbon.

Can Harvard or Oxford or the Sorbonne boast of such successes?

Don't misunderstand. I am not a martyr or hero. I am a journalist and poet (or, as I prefer to think of it, in my heart of hearts, a poet and journalist) who got into trouble with a facetious reference to crocodile tears.

I'm not a poet of political protest. I don't believe in any of that.

I'm a clown, a fellow who horses around. A Portuguese bullfighter—and in Portugal, as you know, the matador doesn't kill the bull.

Which may be worse, of course, for he only annoys the bull before it is led off to an abattoir.

So, because of my ill-considered allusion, I was picked up and interrogated. Not tortured. No electric wires to the genitals, thank you. No brutality in which I was forced to stay awake standing in the infamous statue routine, and not even the terrible box in which, according to reports, the prisoner is unable to stand or sit or lie down but is confined to a painful and eventually permanent crouch. . . .

Of course, those are the things I'd heard about and feared. Those and the possibility of exile to the weird crumbs that are left in the crumbling empire, places of the imagination that are only put onto maps as a kind of jeu d'esprit. I mean, where is São Tomé? Or Timor, or Tarrafal in Cape Verde?

I was once told that there are fictitious places that mapmakers draw onto their productions in order to prevent others from merely copying them and stealing their work. São Tomé might well be one of these. Or the entire Portuguese Empire, for that matter!

On the other hand, what if the PIDE is not the evil group we have been led to expect? What if it is their benevolence that is actually responsible for these dreadful stories—which might well make sense. Assume that the fear of torture is enough to get the cooperation of most prisoners. Would it not make sense to rely on your reputation as a torturer in order to avoid actually torturing anyone?

Most probably, there are rare occasions when, in order to revivify those rumors, they have to torture some ruffian or other.

Dr. Salazar has admitted that on rare occasions a prisoner may have been mistreated, but those who have been badly used, he says, have been "always, or almost always, of the terrorist and extremist category; people who manufactured bombs, and who, in spite of all the questions of the police, refused to reveal where they had hidden their criminal and murderous weapons." And then, quite reasonably, he asked "whether the lives of a defenseless crowd, the lives of little children do not fully justify a little rough handling of half a dozen such wretches."

Can you imagine the bull sessions back at Coimbra, with Salazar and Cerejeira sitting around discussing such nice questions while Dona Maria served them coffee?

Of course, the woman has to be Dona Maria. What would be the point of having an impostor?

The trouble with asking such a question is that while it may very well begin as a purely rhetorical figure, it is apt to turn real. There are actual answers one might make.

As for instance that their intention is to torment Salazar. He can presumably see, can tell that the woman is not his old servant, and even can understand that I am a fraud. The whole idea, then, is to torture Salazar and at the same time to terrify those men who assemble here three mornings a week to pretend to govern the country. Their silence is as necessary as my own, and it would be awkward to kill them.

It wouldn't be impossible, but it would be awkward to kill all of them at the same time. Even the gullible public might notice such a coincidence.

My obvious and inevitable destruction and Salazar's distress— both physical and psychological—are intended to intimidate the old regime and keep them from getting in Caetano's way.

In which case, one must praise Caetano for having learned well the lessons Professor Salazar spent so much time trying to teach his beloved nation.

I have not suffered, myself. Or I have not suffered much. But the fear is nonetheless burdensome. And what makes it all the more difficult is that my fear is not of some extraordinary event, some random accident—that a piano should come crashing down from the rigger's cradle overhead to crush me as I pass by on the sidewalk below, for instance. Life is full of such bizarre events and long-odds risks, and we inure ourselves, learning to accept the perils of existence in a contingent universe, the frailties of the body, the casual possibilities of catastrophe that everywhere abound. But when the fear is of a more intimate nature, when there is intention behind it, when there is no hope of avoiding it by the operation of the laws of chance, then there is a different quality to our lives, a bitterness. . . . It is as if a child were to discover that his parents were unreliable; or, worse, that they hated him and were likely at any moment to turn on him and visit upon him fierce punishments. This is terrible to contemplate, terrible to live with.

And Salazar is like a stern father—an image that he deliberately encourages among the populace of the country. And the state, the corporative state, is like a family from which, however, one cannot escape simply by saying good-bye and marching off from one's village to Lisbon. The choice is between going into exile, which is to leave behind one's land and language, and internal exile, which is to leave one's life, to crawl inside one's shell and hide there, every man his own Anne Frank. And with the PIDE apt to come knocking at the door at any moment of the day or night, one must learn to consider every word, every breath, asking whether this is the one that will give me away, letting them know the awful truth that will give them more than enough reason to condemn me.

This is why Salazar has always spoken of the importance of the family. "When the family breaks up," he has written, "man stands alone before the state, a stranger, defenseless, morally no more than half himself. He loses a name and becomes a number, and social life immediately assumes a different aspect."

Brilliant! You will notice how the ordinary tropes of speech adapt themselves to the harsh realities of the glare of Portuguese sunshine. When is it, after all, that a man loses his name and becomes a number? When he is thrown into prison, of course. So the man's family is the state and the state is his family. To be banished from one is to be ignored and despised by the other.

Blah blah blah blah blah! And what does it all amount to in the end? It is morally uplifting, meliorist, utopian, and crazy. Salazar wants new men, new ideals, and he is willing to sacrifice the old men if need be, the undesirables, the defectives, us poor sods who carry with us the curse of the human condition. "Instead of either superathletes or cripples, let us just have a nation of healthy men and women. Instead of supermen or frightened little men, instead of greedy and nervous men, let us have men with developed wills, calm, patient, and tenacious. In the realm of the intellect, let knowledge be only an infinite capacity for study."

He said it.

I have copied it out, word for word, from the books in the library to which I have access. There is, naturally, a collection of the writings of the great man, which he would expect to hear echoed at every possible occasion by the news broadcasters of his radio station.

A nation of Salazars. A nation of high-minded clerks! All of them wearing those ridiculous black suits, all of them imposing with their modesty and their passive-aggressive good manners, all of them good little boys. . . .

Do you want to know how to breed a tyrant? I will tell you. Take an older couple, a couple that has virtually abandoned hope of a son. Pick a couple that has three or four daughters. And then let the woman conceive a child and let it be a male, to be cosseted and pampered by five adoring women and one astonished old man. The little boy is likely to think he is a king, an emperor, a messiah. He will learn to be a good little boy, quiet and polite. But inside, there will be a yawning chasm of greedy demands that have always been met and had better continue to be met or else he will turn purple and hold his breath and terrorize everyone around him, inflicting the savage penalties of an absolutely unrestrained tyranny.

António de Oliveira Salazar was born on April 28, 1889, in a cottage in the little village of Vimieiro, which is near the town of Santa Comba in the Dão valley between Coimbra and Viseu in the province of Beira Alta. His mother, Maria, was forty-three years old. His father was fifty. The couple already had four daughters, Martha, Elisa, Maria-Leopoldina, and Laura.

And look at him now. He lies there, an insignificant irregularity under the sheets of his pristine bed. His hair is white on the white pillow slip. The bed is a hospital bed they've trucked in, adjustable to all sorts of positions. They ask him if he's comfortable. He blinks once for yes, twice for no.

But what is he really thinking?

He is as mysterious as the writers and painters of Lisbon, having learned at this last stage in his life how to be like them and keep his innermost thoughts to himself. What they do for survival, he is condemned to by his survival.

He has become a Portuguese intellectual, which is to be as mute as a rock in the sunshine, as contorted as a cork tree, almost a part of the landscape but not quite. Not enough. He is still vulnerable.

What I find irresistible is the idea of slipping into these broadcasts some hint of the truth. Let him know that he is no longer the ruler of the country. Let him understand that he has become a toy of Marcello Caetano, that the former servant has now become the master and the old master is reduced to infancy—which is, literally, etymologically, the condition of nonspeech.

As if he were a baby again, but now there are no swarms of adoring sisters and no more indulgent and delighted parents. There is only Dona Maria—and me.

3

THE TEMPTATION IS TO SUPPOSE that there must be reasons. If I am here, performing in this ridiculous and dangerous way, then it must be because I have deserved such a punishment. In this life or another. (So far will the mind wander in order to retain the illusion of orderliness and reason in our chaotic experience.)

By that same token, Salazar must deserve me, and this abject powerlessness into which the foibles of his body and his age have thrust him.

The larger question, though, is whether Portugal deserved Salazar. Was he, after all, no dictator but the humble servant of his country, carrying out our destiny as responsibly as if he had been elected and were answerable at every moment to the peasants of every village, the fishermen of every port, the habitués of every cantina?

Who does not suppose in some part of his mind that the Germans deserved Hitler, that Hitler was an expression (ugly but true enough) of the German heart and spirit? Or that Mussolini, rotund and clownish in that series of bizarre uniforms and funny hats, was not the appropriate expression of the nature of Italians, every bit as fair a sample of their souls as Verdi or Garibaldi?

Pick up any guidebook to Portugal and there will be a simplistic essay—either by some British pundit or by some Portuguese journalist looking to make a few escudos—on the subject of our national character. Invariably you will find the same set of words:

Siso and *loucura*: The former is something like prudence, and the latter is excess, a flair for the quixotic (even though Quixote was Spanish), both of which are presumably at war in the Portuguese soul.

Saudade: This word, also difficult to translate into any other language, suggests our melancholy yearning for past glories. The Greeks, too, have some of this, but they tend to be more cheerful than we. If one were to suppose a Greek at work in his American diner or pizza parlor or resting from his labors on a construction job in Australia but in either case muttering lines from Aeschylus and Sophocles and blaming himself for having fallen from such heights to this present and altogether regrettable condition, then he'd qualify. And there would be a word in Greek that means *saudade*. (But if there is, I'm not familiar with it.)

Sebastianismo: This is the winner, the killer, the one that has most to do with Salazar. This is the secret belief that somehow or other the old days will return, that Sebastian, who was not actually seen to have been killed at Alcácer-Kebir in 1578, is hiding out somewhere and may at any moment turn a corner and come riding down some hill into his old palace courtyard in Lisbon.

The worst of it is that these writers of tourist book essays are correct. Those are the words, and that is the character of our people.

I suppose that another word might be added:

Salazarismo: This means either the belief out there in the country that Salazar may at any moment return to his office and offices. Or, alternatively, Salazar's own belief that he is still running the country.

An Englishman I met once told me that the word most vital to any visitor's understanding of this country was none of the above but the more modest *puxe*, which is pronounced "push" and means "pull."

Without that word, no English-speaking people can get out of the Lisbon airport.

I figure that he's been like this for almost a month. For the first couple of weeks or so, they assumed he'd die. Which would have been convenient. And after that? Their hopes dwindled as he persisted, continued to draw breath, stabilizing and hanging on in this humiliating way.

Humiliating for them, that is. None of them had the nerve to walk in and tell him that there was a new government. And whoever it was who thought up this peculiar charade, the acceptance of the idea was an acknowledgment—shameful and universal—of the lack of nerve of the entire Caetano government.

When they began holding the meetings of the old government in Salazar's bedroom, it soon became clear that there would need to be some semblance of implementation of the decisions they had reached. That was when I was called in. And I assumed that it would be a very temporary kind of duty.

But I've been here more than a week now. Nine days, actually. And I begin to wonder what my prospects are, what possible room I have in which to maneuver.

The Caetano people are my enemies. When Salazar dies, they will resent me and want to do away with me. Salazar, therefore, is my ally.

Some ally.

And yet I have contrived a way to let him know that my reports are false.

It is risky, but unless I take risks I am surely doomed. And with them, I have at least the chance of survival, if only the chance a drowning man sees in the proverbial straws.

Enough straws, and one can make a raft.

In my report this afternoon, I made a passing reference to the Banco de Angola Metropole. It was just a mention, in connection with the career of some minister, who had, I claimed, once been a director of the Banco de Angola Metropole.

There is, of course, no such bank. There never was.

There was, however, a fictional bank of that name, back in the 1920s. It was organized during that chaotic series of governments in order to distribute the half million 500-escudo notes that had been printed up by Waterlow's in England. They weren't counterfeit notes, although that was the result of the scheme. The criminals used the real plates and real paper and then organized a bank in order to launder them into the currency pool.

The scandal was awful. It was a national disgrace that our government was so corrupt, so incompetent, so uncoordinated and feeble as to allow into its middle echelons a group of thieves and swindlers.

On the other hand, men of probity were unlikely to enlist in government service. Between 1918 and 1926, only one president completed his term of office. The rest were killed, or fled in terror, or absconded with whatever funds they could lay their hands on.

It is unlikely that the low-level bureaucrat who has been assigned to monitor my radio broadcasts knows anything about the Banco de Angola Metropole. He might recognize the Waterlow name, but even that's unlikely.

Salazar, on the other hand, would know what I'm talking about. If he knows anything at all.

He is breathing. He may be thinking.

If not . . .?

The above notwithstanding, it is also true that there is a kind of fun in this, that it is entertaining and aesthetically satisfying to introduce nuggets of fiction, satire, extravagance, and absurdity into my very serious reports.

What a wonderful thing for the éminence grise to whisper into the ruler's ear perfectly stupid jokes, dopey rhymes, children's taunts.

The Sun King listens to the presentation of the ambassador

plenipotentiary, then consults for a moment with his own private advisor who leans forward and speaks into his majesty's ear, "Liar, liar, pants on fire."

The only people who can actually talk to Salazar in private are his doctors, his nurses, and Dona Maria.

The doctors report, of course, to Caetano's people.

Only Dona Maria is loyal to the silent and supine man, and it is through her that he will communicate, if he can, and if there is anything he wants to let me know.

The others are very cautious, each of them hoping for some kind of sign, some endorsement from the old man that he could take out to the world to show, and with which he might wrest power from Caetano.

Each of them, wanting that, knows what the others want. And each of them is even more eager to prevent the others from gaining (or claiming) such an advantage than he is to gain it for himself. After all, what can this helpless old man actually do for anyone?

But then, what could one old man ever do? The country looked to him and gave him the powers he exercised. Or not even that. If my recollection of the early history of the New State is accurate, these powers simply fell into his lap.

Unlike the others, Salazar took them seriously, believing in them and even, to a certain extent, exercising them. They became real.

There are moments when I am quite sure that I am fooling myself. The harsh truth is that there is no hope, no hope at all. I'm doomed and will perish within the quarter hour of Salazar's demise. It is only because this reality is so unpleasant that my mind tries to hide from the truth, constructing alternative worlds it would prefer. A ridiculous tactic, but one which would be, in some ways, perfectly appropriate. This is a fantasy country, with our Atlantic fogs the only sure and reliable elements in an otherwise indeterminate landscape.

Dona Maria is an interesting woman to think about. Not that I actually know much about her. On the contrary, she is one of those figures who become famous and whom fame then flattens out into her single known quality. The faithful servant of Salazar's student years, she has been with him ever since.

Interesting that her name is the same as Salazar's mother's.

What is their relationship? It is so much the ideal, or the cliché, as to invite impudent speculation. What arcane perversions can one attribute to these two old wisps of humanity?

Oddly enough, it is easier now that Salazar has been reduced by that blood clot on his brain to the helplessness of the infant a part of him has always wanted to be. He is back in the arms of his surrogate mother. She wipes his brow. She wipes his ass. She croons to him. He listens and his agitation is soothed.

Meanwhile, she is transformed from servant to mistress, empowered by his disability, given the opportunity she must have longed for all this time to return his condescension with her own. Even her acts of kindness, then, have an edge to them.

Her only worry is that he is not altogether aware of these refinements and embellishments.

If he is the simple hulk he appears to be, then he has won.

4

SALAZAR ONCE WROTE that he wanted a regime, "popular but not demagogic, representative but antidemocratic, strong but not tyrannical or all-absorbing."

He missed. What he got was the opposite, demagogic but not popular, antidemocratic and unrepresentative, tyrannical and all-absorbing but not strong.

He had, of course, the problems of the thirties to deal with. It was a time of ogres, with Stalin terrifying on the one side and Hitler, Mussolini, and Franco menacing on the other. And in the middle, there were the ridiculous contortions of the British and the French, for whom political science is nothing more than a hobby. They are essentially ungovernable, both of them, for the British don't need a government and the French don't take any notice of one.

One could discuss in intellectual ways the distinctions between Italian Fascism and the Portuguese *Estado Novo* which was Salazar's invention, the corporative state with its guilds and syndicates, its idea of settling disputes at a round table rather than across a rectangular one.

They are differences that do not make a difference. Dr. Rolão Preto's National Syndicalists wore blue shirts and a Maltese cross instead of the black shirts and the swastika of the National Socialists. Salazar's own Portuguese Legion and Moçidade-Portuguesa were Wehrmacht and Hitler Youth with different uniforms and insignia.

Hitler, Mussolini, Franco, and Salazar were all worried about the Boy Scouts as a hotbed of decadent internationalism. The Boy Scouts and the Freemasons. God knows what they have hidden under their little silk aprons!

In 1932, King Manuel died in England. He'd been living in exile since 1910. His body was brought back to Portugal and he was buried with full honors in the royal tomb. All the fun and none of the mess of monarchy—just showy state funerals.

Lovely! And when the Monarchist *Integralistas* recognized Dom Duarte Nuño of Bragança as the legitimate pretender, Salazar congratulated him and asked for his support. He even declared himself as favoring a Christian monarchy based of course on the corporative state.

Dom Duarte supported Salazar. Salazar never did a thing to restore Dom Duarte to the throne.

It looks as though it ought to be in some operetta or romantic novel. But that was perhaps what troubled Salazar, himself, that his country had broken away from Europe and turned into a setting for Baroness Orczy or Rudolph Friml. Everyone who was anyone spent the day in some café in the Rossio, his employment in some government bureau leaving him substantial amounts of free time because:

  a) he did not know what his duties were;

  b) he would not have been able to perform them, even if he had been told what he was supposed to do;

  c) even if he had performed them, they would have done no good, because there were no plans, no funds, no staff, and no communications;

  d) even if he had been able to perform them and they accomplished what they were supposed to, he'd have been

despised by his colleagues, his family, and his friends for his
unseemly display of energies that were ungentlemanly and made
everyone else look bad.

From 1910 to 1926, there were 9 presidents, 44 ministries,
25 uprisings, 3 dictatorships.

From 1920 to 1925, in Lisbon alone, there were 325 reported
bomb incidents.

There would have been more, but nobody reports bombs that
don't go off. The anarchists were no more efficient than the
bureaucrats.

Often, they were the same people.

In 1926, President Bernardino Machado, accepting the inevitable, invited Mendes Cabeçadas to form a government, abdi-
cated his own office, and fled the Bélem Palace. General
Manuel de Olveira Gomes da Costa met with Cabeçadas in
Sacavém and they sorted out which of them would have what
portfolios.

Cabeçadas proposed to retain for himself the posts of Prime
Minister and Minister of Marine, Justice, and Culture. Gama
Ochoa would have Foreign Affairs and Education. Gomes da
Costa would be Minister for War, for Overseas Territories and
for Agriculture.

Da Costa turned purple. His dignity was affronted. He had
commanded the expeditionary force in Flanders during the
1914 war, those gallant boys whose sacrifice had earned the
fatherland a slice of German East Africa that was tacked on to
Mozambique. He had been that month's savior of the people,
proclaiming the uprising in Braga at the same time as General
Carmona had been proclaiming it in Évora. And now they were
going to stick him in some office and let him worry about
potatoes and wheat blight and that shit?

Go to fucking hell!

Or words to that effect.

Cabeçadas would be Prime Minister and Minister of the
Interior. Da Costa would have War and Overseas Territories

only. (No potatoes! No fucking farms and farmers!) Carmona
could be Foreign Minister.

And for Finance?

There was a promising young economist at the university, a
fellow named Salazar.

Any objections?

No objections.

So they invited Salazar to join the government.

He's thirty-seven years old!

Not quite a kid, but not old, not for a Minister of Finance.
And he'd led a relatively sheltered life, the darling of his family
and then the whiz kid of the university.

He thought the invitation was legitimate. These generals
needed help with the mysteries of finance, and wisely they
turned to one of the experts in their own national university.

Sure, sure, sure.

Never did it cross his mind that finance is where the money
is, that each of them wanted it for himself, that each wanted at
least to keep so juicy a plum out of the hands of the others.

They decided to give it to the kid.

All of them knew that that was a temporary measure.

All, that is, but Salazar.

In one of those Boy's Books of National Heroes, there is a
version of the story it is difficult not to love.

Salazar gets the message back in Santa Comba. He's visiting
his mother, who is dying. (Actually, she died in November,
and this is only June, so it's possible but not quite so dramatic
as our author would have us suppose. But be that as it may.)
The officers who have come up from Sacavém give him the
message and urge him to go to Lisbon at once. He must accept
the portfolio. But the loyal and dutiful son has his responsibili-
ties to his mother.

His mother tells him, "Don't worry about me, son. If they've
come for you, it's because they need you. Accept. The country's rights come before ours. Leave the rest to God!"

I swear I'm not making this up.

If I could make up that kind of thing, I'd never have been

thrown into prison in the first place. I'd be a minister myself. Or a successful writer of Boy's Books of Great Dictators.

So the young man gets up from the bedside where, presumably, he is kneeling, and there is a tear in his eye as he bids farewell to his dear old mum. Off he goes with the officers, wearing his hayseed black suit with the pants too short.

To Lisbon. And history. And greatness!

Well, not right away. Not this time. He goes to the Ministry of the Interior to see Cabeçadas, and then to his own office, and . . .

And nothing. Nobody pays any attention. The phones don't work. And nobody listens to him anyway. The Monarchists and the Republicans are biting each others' asses and Gomes da Costa is making grandiose and irrelevant proposals about decentralization and corporative organization and the restoration of religious education in the schools.

Nobody pays any attention to the kid from Santa Comba. He stamps his foot and says that they've got to listen to him, that he has to be part of the decisions about spending and revenues.

They don't laugh, but only because they are sober and polite men.

The last straw is that Salazar picks up a ringing phone in his office (sometimes they work, at least on incoming calls) and the guy at the other end says he's the Minister of Finance.

As he may have been, the day after the call.

For this, Salazar left his dying mum? For this she sent him off with inspiring words about God and country?

He asks his *chef de bureau* when the next train leaves for Coimbra.

"In two hours, Excellency!"

Salazar is on that train.

Humiliating, of course. And you can see where the impetus comes for his later career.

All those groans of pain in Mozambique and Angola are the payment for that old humiliation. All the PIDE tortures are a part of the reparations for that insult of 1926.

Never again would that happen to him. No, never would he be humiliated by powerlessness and irrelevance.

Salazar writes: "In order to understand the Portuguese problem, we must regard it in its true perspective, when amidst conditions of unrest, impoverishment, and dissension Europe was groping for a solution to her own political difficulties. The imputation that the Dictatorship was instituted as a result of a so-called 'barrack-room plot' in order that a military clique might gain control of the Government shows a complete ignorance of the general ill feeling prevalent in the country, of the tendencies of the time, and of the weakness, submissiveness, and shortcomings of successive governments: conditions which one might perhaps describe as a 'crisis of a modern State'."

Blah, blah, blah.

What he's saying is that this is never going to happen again. I'll fix these guys!

Fucking Portuguese!

I announced on this evening's news program that Gomes da Costa won a prize for growing the largest hog in the Beira Alta province.

Salazar? Are you there? Are you listening, old hog?

It must have been frustrating, after all that effort, to look around and realize that all you were dictator of was this tiny country where nothing has happened for three hundred years. Where there are a number of people waiting for Sebastian to return.

And those are the intellectuals.

The others are too dumb to have heard of Sebastian in the first place.

Pope Leo XIII said, in *Rerum Novarum*, "Inasmuch as the domestic household is antecedent, as well in idea as in fact, to the gathering of men into a community, the family must necessarily have rights and duties which are prior to those of the community and founded more immediately in nature."

To which Salazar replied, "Sure thing, fella! I'll take a piece of that."

Apologists for Salazar have argued that Leonine teaching allows for any kind of government, provided only that it does not infringe on basic human rights. On that principle, Salazar's corporative state is not inherently objectionable.

True enough, but the argument misses the real point, because there was no other way for him to give them back what they deserved for the way they'd let him go in 1926.

They hadn't even bothered to dismiss him. They'd simply ignored him and let him slink away like a begging cat from a table in one of those cafés.

Two months later, Carmona throws da Costa out on his ear for corruption, greed, and terminal incompetence, and only because it would be humiliating to the country to have one of its generals locked up in jail is da Costa allowed to sneak away to an exile in the Azores.

At Coimbra, Salazar, hearing about this, would have been pleased.

Not satisfied, maybe, but pleased.

5

THERE WAS A CABINET MEETING this morning. They came troop-
ing in, carrying their dispatch cases and looking like perfectly
serious *hommes d'affaires*.

It is almost enough to restore my faith in mankind, for I
know that this is all sham, that these are clowns, that they are
pretending, playing like little boys, as irrelevant to the actual
workings of the government as . . . as I am! And their sober
faces only make the comedy richer, more sophisticated, more
biting.

There is a long table in dark wood, mahogany I suppose, at
which they sit, probably in the same places they are accustomed
to from their meetings in the palace. And they discuss, in
perfect seriousness, the issues of the day. They are briefed, I
assume, by some junior clerk from the actual Ministry, so they
have plausible subjects for their ongoing performances. I am in
attendance, dressed as a clerk, cautioned not to open my
mouth—Salazar might recognize my voice.

This is how I find out what is happening in the fantasy world
they are governing.

The hardest pressed is probably António Gonçalves Rapazote,
who had recently replaced Alfredo dos Santos as Minister of the
Interior and was therefore in charge of the PIDE, which is one

of the regime's mainstays. He who is supposed to be the master of the secret police has become their victim. And the psychology of the victim is rather different from that of the captor and tormentor.

João Augusto Dias Rosas has a hard row to hoe, too. He is Salazar's Finance Minister, and finance is what Salazar knows best. So he has to be on his mettle.

The others mostly agree, assent, occasionally ask an obvious question. There must be threats Caetano has made, or intimations of unpleasantness that the PIDE has managed in its laconic way to convey. These are family men. They have given hostages to fate. What happens to those hostages is up to them and how well they behave.

Who would want his daughter to disappear? Who would be comfortable supposing—at the best—that she had been sold into white slavery and was now thrashing about under Amazonian savages in some primitive Brazilian crib?

So they debate and discuss. And mostly they report good news. The Alentejo project is a great success now that the Roxo Dam is operating. The question—a fine question, for it can be debated almost endlessly—is whether the industrial growth is sufficient to warrant a further extension of medium- and long-term credits or whether this would have too inflationary an impact on the national economy.

There are thoughtful discussions of these matters.

Nobody laughs.

Nobody even ventures to write jokes on the pads set out before each of the places with three newly sharpened pencils and a filled glass of ice water.

They just discuss. And they drink the water. They drink lots and lots of water.

When we all leave, I suppose Salazar and Dona Maria review the event.

He asks questions and she answers them.

Or perhaps she asks questions and he answers them.

Or, for all I know, there are no discussions. She is pretending, too, so that she can keep her place here. What kind of job can an eighty-five-year-old servant expect to find, after all?

Wouldn't it be wonderful if Salazar were as inert as a slab of dried cod in a fishmonger's shop and Dona Maria were only pretending to interpret his winks and twitches!

Thousands of escudos wasted because some mean clerk refused to approve the minuscule pension she was supposed to have!

But it is also possible that she is the faithful servant performing her tasks as well as she can, given her age and her physical and mental limitations, which are considerable.

In which case, if he asks her questions, either about inconsistencies he has noticed or slips the shadow cabinet may have made, she has no possible way of answering him. She has no more idea what is real and what is imaginary than any peasant.

Which is, actually, the Portuguese problem, one that Salazar has never been able to solve.

When Salazar went away, there must have been laughter and, perhaps, relief. Such a serious young man! And such a woeful suit—always the same one.

Carmona—Marshal António Óscar de Fragoso Carmona, President of the Republic—forgot about Salazar, or would have liked to. But Salazar kept popping up in annoying ways. He published articles in *Novidades* based on what he had learned about the national accounts during his brief stay at the Ministry.

It was a scandal, of course, and that surprised no one. What was unusual was that Salazar had the skills of a bookkeeper and had pored over the ledgers, understanding those columns of figures and making sense of them. Or understanding that they made no sense, were an affront to sense and probity and fiscal responsibility.

And speeches. He gave speeches about political economy and the need for hard work as the only reasonable basis of economic development. Hard work on the one hand and the regulation of consumption on the other.

What any bookkeeper could understand.
Or any peasant.
He was, Carmona thought, becoming a pest.

So, at that point, Carmona having expressed his annoyance, some eager underling would very probably have set to work investigating Salazar's brief tenure in the Ministry of Finance. I'm just guessing, of course, but it seems more than likely, does it not? The man had become an embarrassment and needed to be shut up. How better to do that than to expose some peculation, some infraction, some conflict of interest. . . .

And in the real world, one expects to find such things, for no one is clever enough to hide all his tracks all the time.

But nothing. No evidence of any wrongdoing of any kind. He didn't take so much as a yellow pad from the stationery cabinet. Not a pencil. Not even the nameplate that had been made for his desk and that was of no use to anyone else, unless of course his name also happened to be Dr. António de Oliveira Salazar.

Governmental operations being what they are, word of the results of this inquiry gets back to Carmona, who wonders whether Salazar is a maniac or a moron.

Or a genius?

No, there aren't geniuses! Not in this world.

Not, at any rate, in Portugal.

And outside? Demonstrations and disorders. Riots, really, but that is an inflammatory word antagonistic reporters are likely to use whenever three or more ruffians meet at random on a street corner.

Still, 80 people were killed in Oporto alone, with 360 injured.

In Lisbon, more than 100 died.

In the last four months of 1927, 635 people were exiled.

Not what even sympathetic reporters would call an overwhelming show of support for the government and its policies.

And looking down from his window in the Presidential Palace, Carmona must have thought from time to time about that

hick from Coimbra with the short trouser legs that showed
swaths of pale calf above the socks.

They still had that goddamn nameplate.

Maybe that was why he'd left it behind?

On March 25, 1928, Carmona was confirmed as President of
the Republic and began what was supposed to be a seven-year
term. It would have been hard to find anyone in Lisbon willing
to bet that Carmona would last seven months.

Or seven weeks, for that matter.

He sent Duarte Pacheco, his Minister of Education, to Coimbra
to invite Salazar to rejoin the government. And, if need be, to
negotiate, a professor persuading a professor.

I cannot decide whether the instructions would have been
required to be put into words. I like to think so, but only
because, as a poet, I am fond of words and of their sounds in
the ear and their textures on the tongue.

"What should I give him?" Pacheco might well have said.

Carmona would have looked down from his window at the
pedestrians who, at any instant, could turn into rioters and
revolutionaries. (There is only so much that human beings will
put up with—even Portuguese!) And he might have said, "Whatever he wants."

Or he might not have said anything at all but just held out
his hands, palms up.

At least he would find out the answer to the question that
had been bothering him for so long, whether Salazar was the
maniac or the moron. Or the genius.

The question is still open, for that matter.

Turning once again to the Boy's Book of Despots, we read of
the encounter: "Salazar asked for a night to think it over, and
he spent much of this night on his knees, in church, like a
squire on the vigil of knighthood."

No shit!

From Salazar's own mouth, the story is only slightly less
preposterous: "I hesitated all night. I did not know if I should
accept the proposition that had been made to me. I was terribly

depressed at the idea of leaving the University. I foresaw the possibility of failure. Imagine, if I had failed to put the finances in order, what would my students have thought of me?"

What, indeed? But then, failure would not have seemed to him anything more than a remote possibility. Not a probability, surely. And he must also have imagined that university admiration to which he'd become accustomed extending to a somewhat larger arena. Not the whole world, maybe, but at least the whole of Portugal.

Salazarismo's first-known manifestation!

The bargaining with Pacheco was rather less highfalutin, evidently. What Salazar insisted upon at the minimum were these four understandings:

1) No government department should exceed in its expenditures the amount authorized to it by the Ministry of Finance.

2) No government department should take any action affecting the state's receipts or expenditures without first having obtained the agreement of the Ministry of Finance.

3) The Ministry of Finance shall have a veto over all increases of current or ordinary expenditure, and no special or developmental expenditures should be undertaken without the Ministry of Finance first being informed.

4) Measures for the reduction of expenditures and for the collection of revenues shall be organized on uniform principles and all departments shall collaborate with the Ministry in cooperation in these efforts.

Not surprisingly, Pacheco agreed. When he returned to Lisbon, he reported to Carmona, who asked the correct question. "He had these points worked out beforehand?"

Pacheco believed so.

Carmona shook his head. "He will save the country or else drive it into the sea."

"Yes, Excellence."

"We'll know in a year. Or even sooner."

Pacheco nodded.

◆

At his installation, Salazar made a little speech in which he described his decision to resume his duties as Minister of Finance. "Such a sacrifice," he said, "I could never have undertaken . . . just for the sake of obliging someone. It is a sacrifice which I am willing to make for my country, in serene and calm discharge of a conscientious duty."

What it doesn't say in the Boy's Book of Tyranny, but what is obvious and depressing, is that it is necessary to have read exactly that kind of book and, even worse, to believe it. To have swallowed it, hook, line, and sinker.

He may very well have spent an hour or so on his knees in some goddamn church, just so he could have that written about him one day and know that it wasn't a lie.

Knights don't lie, after all, do they?

Not if they don't absolutely have to.

Poets, on the other hand, do lie. Like bandits. Whenever we possibly can.

Lies like truth, as the phrase goes.

The polite word for it is fiction. But you and I know that the truth of the matter in plain and unadorned language is lies. Falsehoods.

Inventions sounds neutral, but to be neutral is already to have taken sides.

Those who are not for us are against us. If you are not part of the solution, then you are part of the problem.

To the barricades!

In my news report—one hesitates to call it a broadcast if it is cast only into the one loudspeaker in the radio on Salazar's nightstand—I referred to the unmasking of an impostor at the Sisters of Mercy Hospital in Estoril, a fellow who wanted to play at doctor as he had probably done when he was a naughty young lad just emerging from latency's chrysalis.

His talents and personality, however, were unsuited to the rigors of medical education. So he just ignored that part of it, found himself a white coat and a stethoscope, and began prowling the wards, announcing to patients who caught his eye that he was a doctor and examining them.

According to the reports of these patients, his manner was friendly and concerned, and his medical suggestions were conservative and sensible.

Still, it is against the law to masquerade as a physician. He has been sentenced to two years in prison—where, I have no doubt, he will be assigned to hospital duties in which he will perform admirably.

I reported this story accurately enough. The only thing I changed was the name. And a little of the background.

The impostor's name, I said, was Duarte Pacheco. He admitted to having been an impostor and practical joker for years—indeed, that he'd begun as early as 1928.

The poor pimply PIDE kid who has been assigned to monitor my announcements would hardly be likely to recognize Pacheco's name.

On the other hand, if Salazar hadn't already had a stroke, this might have caused one.

6

So there he is in Lisbon, working away in the Ministry of Finance, and he's not a maniac and he's not a moron, and he's certainly not a genius.

What he is, amazingly enough, is an unobtrusive little drudge, a superclerk, the kind of man who'd make a terrific librarian, maybe.

Or even better, make him the manager of a plumbing supply warehouse, the kind of man who knows where every washer and spigot and valve and spit cock is piled, and how many of them there are, and what they cost, and which ought to be reordered, and what you can use to substitute for it if you're out of something. Those legendary long hours he puts in at his desk are probably true. And embarrassing. That passion for detail he's supposed to have is the hallmark of a nonexecutive.

What made him our great national leader, then? What he did was to express us, simply by being so splendidly unoriginal, so perfectly banal. If you were to have gone out and interviewed a random sampling of old guys in a café, a gathering of merchants or landowners, say, or a few laborers out on a break, you would have found the same opinions, the same pieties, the same prejudices.

That dreadful suit of his was cut from the cloth of all of Portugal.

The only difference was that he had a kind of economic policy, which wasn't very sophisticated either, but he knew the right words to use. And he seemed so stern when he talked about the suppression of the ad valorem tax and the consolidation of credits.

Nobody knew what those things meant.

But that meant that nobody was likely to care enough to argue with him about such subjects.

More to the point was his speech of 21 October 1929, when he assumed dictatorial powers, or, more accurately, when the nation realized that his conditions of acceptance of the Ministry of Finance amounted to an assumption of dictatorial powers. This speech was entitled "A Policy of Truth, A Policy of Sacrifice, A National Policy."

What he called for was an end to the lies—an end to the thefts of payrolls with no workers, courts with no cases, schools with no students, under-the-table tax deals, bribes, and the wholesale swindle that had been in effect since 1910. "The policy of truth calls . . . for drastic changes in this state of affairs."

What he was most deeply upset about was that Portugal was a laughingstock of Europe.

That's what Mussolini worried about in Italy, too.

In the Europe of the first half of the twentieth century, however, to be a laughingstock was no dishonor.

Look at the serious countries and what they were up to!

I'm not about to set forth a military and political history of Europe from 1928 to 1968. It's not necessary. But there is room for an observation here and there.

As with Spain, for instance, and the *Pacto Iberico* of 1939.

It is simple enough to say that Franco was a Fascist, that Salazar was a Fascist, and that therefore they made a pact and that was it, no problem, good-bye.

But Salazar also had a pact with England, which has been our ally since John of Gaunt's time. (*Sebastianismo* has its occasional advantages, you see.)

And you've also got to understand Portuguese pride. The integrity of the national boundaries, and all that. Who would want to divide up the tiny country of Portugal?

Ah, but that's just it. Look at the Basques. Catholics mostly, but they were nevertheless Republicans (i.e. Commies) because they were really separatists, and they wanted to run their own affairs. They considered the Republicans as their likelier allies. The Republicans were internationalists, and they thought Pan-Iberianism was just fine. Under Franco, Spain would stay together, one big ugly entity in which the Basques and their interests would be ignored. Under a Republican government, a weak and silly association of debaters, utopians, do-gooders, aristocrats-gone-wrong, and stooges of Litvinov, the Basques would make out pretty well. And if Portugal were annexed on the west, the Basque country in the east would be almost an equivalent, nearly independent.

What Salazar saw in all this was the Balkanization of Iberia.

First Spain and then Portugal.

A whole bunch of itty-bitty duchies and principalities and republics as if it were the thirteenth century again.

Not a bad century, actually. Except for the Moors.

Or, depending on your point of view, the Christians.

It's tough to disagree with him, actually. If Spain and Portugal had broken up into those itty-bitty city-states, what do you think would have happened during World War II? France was not exactly the bastion of Europe that would protect us all.

Look at the Netherlands. Look at Belgium. Look at Denmark.

Salazar knew our state of preparedness, and he figured we might hold out for thirty-seven seconds.

It takes that long to run up a white flag, even if you hurry.

So he wasn't a democrat. There was a literacy rate of thirty-five percent—if you believe the government figures. Cut that in half for a more realistic estimate. No terrific base for all those fine democratic institutions. I mean, what he was running was essentially a joke country.

With an empire, of course. The fifth largest empire in the world. Goa and Macao and those big blobs in Africa, Angola and Mozambique. Not to mention the Azores and the Madeiras and Timor and a lot of other far-flung dots.

Those were as much a part of Portugal as the Minho or the Algarve. Surely, they were as much a part of Portuguese honor. The fruits of those epic adventures, the yield of those heroic exploits!

The blacks, the colonials, were like children, but then so were the peasants of Trás-Os-Montes e Alto Douro.

Or, put it another way. If you cede independence to those large swaths of Africa, Portugal becomes that joke country Salazar always feared it might be.

Take away those colonies, and the dream is over. The bubble is pricked.

The difference between Salazar and the other dictators is less a matter of character than of situation and sheer opportunity. It's luck as much as anything else. If you'd taken Stalin or Hitler or Mussolini, plucked them up from where they were and given them Portugal instead, how much trouble could any of them have caused?

On the other hand, Salazar in the Kremlin or the Bunker or that balcony over the Piazza Venezia would have been relatively benign.

No great claim, maybe, but still, a part of the story.

Another modest claim is that he didn't invent Africa. Or discover it. It was there, had been there, almost forever—as a part of Portugal.

The British, the French, the Germans, the Belgians, the Italians, they were all arrivistes. And they brought with them condescending ideas of how the natives should be treated. We were sincere in our expectations that they would be happy to be a part of Portugal, that they would welcome the very real benefits of civilization, that they would be our brothers.

Also our wives and our children.

As in Brazil, for instance. Or the Cape Verde islands. Or the Azores. Or Goa.

We are not racists. Or even, in the pattern of those other countries, imperialists.

What a disappointment, then, to have these tribes in Angola and Mozambique rejecting us.

Worst of all, the ones who had most benefited from our presence, the educated ones, the city dwellers, the ones we most expected to be black-skinned Portuguese, they were the malcontents who wanted Angola for the Angolans.

There was no such country. There never had been any such entity. There were a bunch of savages, prancing about, killing one another, the Luba and the Lunda and the Kasanje, and the Matamba, and the Ndonga and the Bailundu and the Loango, and of course the Kongo, who are better known because of the river and the territory the Belgians took from us.

We came, before anyone else, and we settled there, trading and working. We carved out a territory in which we built roads and railways, turned the jungle into a garden, brought sanitation and education and religion. . . .

Who does not believe in these things?

On 20 June 1960, Salazar proclaimed: "Portugal will never agree to discuss self-determination for its overseas territories."

In Angola, Father Pinto de Andrade expressed his disagreement with Salazar's position and was arrested by the PIDE. He was thrown into the same jail with Father Agostinho Neto on Conakry. Members of the MPLA (never mind these initials, all of which are so much alphabet soup—these happen to stand for Angolan Popular Liberation Movement) organized a demonstration to demand the liberation of the two priests. Troops opened fire on them, killing thirty and injuring about two hundred.

What made this a particularly impressive confrontation was that the military had replaced the police.

And this was no gang of Luanda riffraff but country people, cotton pickers mostly, the quiet ones.

◆

Of course, by then, any fool could have seen that there was no reasonable solution left. That there was no middle ground.

We had brought them Christianity, which is a fine religion. What they had picked up from it was a fondness for crucifixion.

A lot of whites and mestiços (mulattos) were crucified. On the other hand, a lot of blacks had electrodes attached to their genitals, which is the European fad in torture.

A demonstration of the respect we have for power of one kind or another.

Salazar said it was the work of outside agitators, mostly from the Congo, and Communists.

That's what all entrenched authorities say.

Except that Salazar was probably right.

But that made no difference. Sometimes, being right isn't enough.

He never went there. He hardly ever went anywhere. He just sat at his desk and imagined it, or more likely, tried not to imagine it, tried not to think about it.

As if it were a bad dream.

In a way, it was. It made no more sense than a dream. One of those dumb incidents, unpredictable and in itself all but meaningless, but in retrospect decisive.

The fifteenth of March, 1961, and the laborers of the Primavera plantation demanded an increase in their wages. As workers are apt to do.

And the owner refused, as owners are apt to do, too.

And the workers rebelled!

And the owner put down the rebellion with rifles and shotguns, there being so many more of the workers than there were of the owners and managers.

The revolt spread to other plantations, all over Angola. The Angolese wanted suddenly to be freed from the oppression of their masters, to break the chains of their servitude.

And who could tell them they were wrong?

All the world looked on in sympathy. Slavery tends to be unpopular and exploitation is unsympathetic.

Only the Portuguese knew these people well enough to understand that if you didn't force them to work, they wouldn't work at all but go back to their dirty little villages and sit around the communal huts drinking palm wine and singing epics, while their women worked in the fields.

They were slavers themselves, slave owners and slave traders, and they didn't like anyone else exercising what they took to be their own prerogatives.

None of those Iron Curtain propagandists ever mentioned any of that, as if that were all irrelevant and beside the point.

It probably was. Irrelevant and beside the point.

Salazar knew he was right. That was enough for him. It all added up, like the sums of columns of figures.

And he found himself suddenly promoted up to the seriousness of a Hitler or a Mussolini or a Stalin.

Not the star, maybe, but a member of the team. A serious player, if you judge seriousness by sheer quantities of human blood.

A British journalist said that the fighting in Angola was worse than the Mau Mau uprisings in Kenya had been. Thousands of Africans joined the nationalists, many of them because they were afraid not to. The atrocities that the natives figured out for those who refused to join them were "indescribable."

On the other hand, the government forces were trying to burn the jungle clean and were using napalm to destroy villages. One Portuguese air force officer said, "We hunt the terrorists down like game."

Dr. Adriano Moreira, the Overseas Minister, admitted that punitive raids were being made on villages that were "suspected of harboring terrorists."

The PIDE organized "psychosocial" services to "pacify disaffected portions of the population." As many as ten thousand of these "disaffected" people were interned at Moçâmedes.

A nightmare.

I look at him and wonder what his dreams are like.

7

FROM WHAT I AM ABLE TO GATHER, it seems that Salazar fell—in a perfectly literal way—after having been treated by his chiropodist at his summer villa on the road between Lisbon and Estoril. It is interesting to imagine what the chiropodist could have done, cut too deeply, or perhaps used some anesthetic? At any rate, Salazar fell down and hit his head. There was a clot that developed.

The clot affected him, as apparently they are able to do, confusing him, making him at the same time sleepy and querulous.

He was upset by his confused state, but he nevertheless agreed to surgery, which was performed by Dr. Marques, prominent neurosurgeon and oppositionist, with Dr. Lima assisting and Salazar's old friend and personal physician Dr. Eduardo Coelho looking on.

The operation was a success, but the patient had a massive stroke twenty-four hours later.

And he has been like this ever since, unable to recover but refusing to die.

My occasional inventions and embellishments have not seemed to bother him. They have not had any effect one way or another, or so I thought. But this morning, when I was walking in the garden, Dona Maria came out with her pruning shears to collect new flowers for the faience vase on the bureau across from the patient's bed, where he may nor may not notice them.

"You!" she said, in what appeared to be a vocative of direct address.

"Yes?"

"He knows."

"He knows? He knows what?"

"He knows. He wanted me to tell you. And that he thanks you."

"What do you mean?" I asked.

She shrugged. She was unwilling or unable to expatiate. She was delivering his message. She turned away and resumed her inspection of the flower beds and her quest for suitable blossoms.

And he thanks me?

But of course! Whatever my intentions may have been, the result is that I have let him know that my broadcasts are a charade, a parody of the news rather than the news itself. It is a question of literary genres. I have let him know he is involved now not in drama or even melodrama but farce.

If I had been his friend, his faithful and devoted admirer, I could have not done better for him!

Fooling around, I have let him see that they are all trying to fool him, too. That those cabinet meetings are charades. That their decisions are nonsense. That the government is elsewhere.

The man is immobilized and inexpressive—aphasia, I think, is the word they use for his condition—but he is not insentient. And he's got nothing else to do but lie there and think.

If I'm sending nonsense out into his radio, then that's got to be accounted for. The whole country cannot have been taken over by some modernist playwright or trendy novelist. Therefore, the country is going its own way out there and he is in here, with these men . . .

All of whom have betrayed him!

◆

Only I have been loyal.

Nothing could have been farther from my intention. I wanted to inflict pain on the man. To punish and humiliate him.

He is responsible for this grotesque semblance of a government we have. He is responsible for the PIDE and its cruelties and barbarisms, and he is ultimately responsible for my having been put into jail for a very nearly innocent reference in a poem that no more than two hundred people would have been likely to read. Crocodile tears isn't even original, except in the context of those stories from Angola.

Of course, by having put me in jail, the PIDE has made me and that poem relatively famous—at least as poems in Portuguese go, these days. Not those windy failed epics of our tradition but the shorter lyric. Or satire.

And for this unintentional favor, I have repaid Dr. Salazar with another even greater favor.

For which he thanks me!

Lord, lord, lord!

What is wonderful to think about is whether he will contrive to let his ministers know that he knows, to make them all understand that he has seen through their imposture. He knows them to be the sorry little toadies they truly are. What can they do? Quit?

They would then have to answer to Caetano, and then to the PIDE eventually.

Whatever humiliation Salazar can devise for them, they will have no choice but to accept it, and smile, too, and say thank you.

Just as he has thanked me.

Yes, just so.

It has taken me a while, but I have come to understand that this is no joking matter. Salazar may not be able to do anything more than ruin us all—his cabinet and, quite incidentally, me, too. He has nothing to fear for himself. What can they do to him? They could kill him, of course, but that would be doing him a favor.

But the others, the old men who have been coming in every day with their attaché cases and their portfolios and their smiles and their lies . . . they will rebel! He will try to humiliate them and they will walk away.

Better yet, they will jump up and down, making faces like naughty children and telling him what they always thought of him. They will stick out their tongues and hold their hands up to their heads, putting their thumbs in their ears and wiggling their fingers.

But in the end, they will leave him, walk out of this fantasy and back into the real world.

And Salazar will have solitude, the isolation the PIDE is said to use on certain political detainees.

I will be less fortunate. It will come out somehow that it was through my stupid jokes that Salazar discovered the truth. I'll be blamed. And I'll be punished.

Electrodes and bastinadoes.

And, eventually, death.

In the very unlikely event that anyone ever learns of my demise, it could happen that I'd become one more martyr to the Portuguese tyranny.

Which is all right. I don't mind being a martyr. But it wouldn't be true. And while impostures and ironies are okay in literature, they get to be a pain in the ass after a while in life.

One wants something simple and real and unduplicitous.

One is childish, of course. There are no such things.

Not in Portugal, anyway.

Perhaps if I can persuade Dona Maria of the dangers, I may yet be able to retrieve my folly or avoid some of its dire consequences.

So what if he does know? If nobody else knows that he knows, it won't matter. And she is the one who interprets his blinks and twitches. Or claims to be doing that.

If they just stick him away in some hospital ward and leave him to rot, it would serve him right. And they could, too. They could let his beard grow. Or maybe just his mustache. A great big joke mustache—like Stalin's. But that wouldn't be good for Dona Maria. She's got a good thing going here. I shall appeal to her self-interest and sense of self-preservation.

And of course it will be in vain, because she is that impossibly admirable and impossibly stupid peasant female Salazar might have been expected to pick, a woman whose loyalty is so great as to take precedence over any impulse toward self-preservation.

She will do what he tells her, no matter how disastrous. Just out of obedience and dumb honor.

Shit!

Perhaps I have been too pessimistic. It could well be that Salazar will be satisfied with a kind of humiliation of his ministers. He will perhaps require of them only that they agree with him as he comes to increasingly bizarre decisions to which they would have to give their assent. To have to come to the palace every day and pretend to govern is one thing, but to have to appear to accept insane policies and ridiculous new regulations is quite another.

The value of the escudo should not be allowed to fluctuate but should represent a true value of some staple of the economy. The value of the escudo should represent the retail price of a can of sardines.

"Sim. Seguramente!"

For that matter, cans of sardines can be used as currency. Why not? They're much less messy than grapes or olives, and they last longer than loaves of bread.

"Maravilhoso!"

And the way to solve the illiteracy problem of Portugal is to decree that the official language of Portugal will be pictures.

"Bravo!"

But would that be enough?

I doubt it. He is enraged. He is infuriated, first of all, by the betrayal of his trusted advisors and ministers, but that must be only a small matter compared to his larger rage—at his disability itself. For a man of such power to be so suddenly and cruelly

reduced cannot be easy to accept. He cannot revenge himself
on God or the fates or on his physicians, or even on Dona
Maria for that matter—but his ministers are there, good for
nothing else, deserving of whatever tortures he can contrive for
them. He is not likely to be satisfied by childish practical jokes.

Dona Maria approached me again this morning in the gar-
den. "You are to say nothing of what we spoke about last time."
"He told you to tell me that?" I asked her.
She nodded.
"All right," I said. "I won't say anything. You can assure
him."
"And for your safety, you need not continue your signals to
him."
"I understand," I told her.
She nodded again and scurried away.
Perhaps then he will do nothing?
I don't believe it, not for a moment. Nothing that good or
that easy could happen to me.
Poets are supposed to be the speakers of truth—but that is
not necessarily to our credit. I think it may just be that every-
one else is smart enough to know when to keep his big mouth
shut.

8

_____

THERE WAS A CABINET MEETING this afternoon. The members of the cabinet took their seats, and Senhor Lopes, the Deputy Chairman of the Council of Ministers, called the meeting to order. I was seated at a small table in a corner, beyond the large council table. At the other end of the room, Salazar lay in his bed, staring vacantly at the ceiling.

Dona Maria came into the room to take her place at Salazar's bedside and interpret for the rest of us his winks and grimaces. She was wearing her usual black dress, black shawl, and black shoes, but she carried a clipboard, which was something new. I noticed it but thought nothing much of it until she cleared her throat and interrupted the Council of Ministers, which was not something I'd ever seen her do before.

"Dr. Salazar has asked me to make an announcement," she told them.

They were surprised but attentive.

"Yes? Please!" Senhor Lopes was smiling, encouraging the simple woman, trying to put her at her ease and show her every consideration.

Dona Maria drew herself up to her full five feet and held the clipboard out in front of her. Apparently, she is farsighted. She read from the notes before her: "Dr. Salazar has asked me to tell

you that he understands what has been happening. He is aware
that there is another government outside this room—and that
you have all betrayed him. He has asked me to announce to
you that he forgives you. He understands that you would not
have done such a thing except under duress. He wants me to
say to you that he forgives you, one and all, and will repay good
for evil. He will not betray you. We must all continue with this
arrangement. But he wants each of you to swear to secrecy—
not for his sake anymore but for your own sakes. Each of you
must resist the temptation to run to the new authorities and try
to be the first one to bring them the news that their charade
has been exposed. You must swear loyalty to one another and
each of you must promise on his honor to keep his secret
hidden deep within his breast. Finally, he asks of you that,
once you have obliged him in this way, you continue to transact the business of the Council as you have been doing and
would have done, had he not made this discovery of his known
to you. It is the only way to protect your own safety and that of
your loved ones and your friends."

There was a moment of shock and astonishment. And then
Senhor Rosas, the Finance Minister, turned on Dona Maria
and accused her of having made it all up. "I don't believe it,"
he said, "not for a minute! He couldn't have said all that. He
can't talk!"

"He can say yes and no. I ask questions and he answers
them," she said perfectly calmly.

"And what did you ask him? Whether he knows that these
meetings are those of the actual government? Whether he knows
that there is now another government?"

"I asked him only whether he was upset. What was troubling
him? He thinks of a word and I have to guess it. I call out
letters and he tells me whether I have the right word or not."

"Impossible," Senhor Veiga insisted. Senhor Veiga is Minister of Planning—or used to be.

"I asked whether he was upset because of the Council, and
he said yes. And then he made me guess a word. The word
was Judases. And I asked him which ones, and he told me
all of you."

There was a lively discussion, full of the actual passion and controversy that they have been trying to simulate all this time. But the upshot was that they swore not to betray one another.

Whether this is useful or really changes anything is another question, of course. They were all Judases—by their own admission. Are they likely to have reformed much in so short a period of time?

On the other hand, they are now afraid of each other. And they all look to Salazar for leadership. Or in fear of what he yet may do.

My confidence of yesterday has ebbed. I spent a dreadful night, tossing and turning, unable to sleep, and then, when I did succumb to exhaustion, tormented by vivid dreams of imprisonment.

I am imprisoned now, of course, but it is a comfortable life, a privileged existence to which I have too quickly become accustomed. I am terrified of losing this and of being returned not to my previous incarceration but to something far worse—the labor camps on São Tomé or Timor or wherever they have them, wasting away as I toil in the soap mines, as the hot sun beats down.

Not even that prospect—which is real enough—makes the jokes go away. But then, the jokes don't make my situation any the less dangerous.

It was a bold move that Salazar made, but it is doomed to failure. At least one of those men must be an informer for the PIDE. Maybe two or three. Or perhaps they all are.

Salazar's insult—that each might very probably try to be the first to report to the PIDE—was too optimistic. The truth of the matter is that in all probability each will hurry to make his report in the hope that he is not the last man to do so.

But perhaps Salazar is aware of that, too?

What a frail vessel in which we have placed our hopes!

But that was always true, even before the fall and the stroke! It is always the case in any dictatorship. What a frail vessel is any individual into which a nation agrees to entrust its destiny!

◆

On the other hand, having written the foregoing, I am not satisfied. My guess is that the appearance of feebleness will be enough to put at least a few of the cabinet ministers off their guard. And that is what Salazar may be counting on. All he needs is for there to be a rift in their uniformity, a division among them, and he can exploit that somehow, as he has been able to do so many times before. He is not spectacular in the manner of other twentieth-century autocrats, but it is also true that he has held onto his power as few of the others have been capable of doing. He has the limitations of mortality, but to those he has not added any additional impediments such as recklessness or stupidity. He is at heart a realist—which is why it must be so grievous an affront to be thrust into this official fantasy and put at the head of an unreal regime.

If I were forced to bet, or allowed to, I'd bet on Salazar rather than on these silly men who sit at the table and pretend—to him, to one another, and to themselves.

Of course, there may be a way for me to do some such thing. I have begun to have a glimmer of a plan.

It is not Salazar's plan, but then I don't have the advantage he presently enjoys of having so little to lose. I am young, relatively speaking, still in love with life, and I should be most sorry to miss the chance of reading the poems I could produce in the span that ought to remain to me.

The great thing that he's seen is that there is a kind of pride that Caetano shares with all Portuguese and it is a vulnerability. He does not want to be humiliated and cannot stand to be made to appear ridiculous.

This is not so inestimable a weapon as it may appear. Salazar, I rather suspect, has seen a way to wield it.

And in a modest way, so have I.

I left a note for one of the younger cabinet members on the second page of his writing tablet where the chances were better than even that he'd find it. He is a man whom I cannot identify, for reasons that will become clear, but I had noticed that he doodles a lot during these meetings. My message for him on that second page said: "Senhor, it is urgent that we talk privately. Go to the *lavatório* and I will follow you there."

There was no signature. But my expectation was that his curiosity or his fear would be enough to prompt him into action. And during the course of the morning's session he did indeed get up and go off to the men's room—either in compliance with the instruction or in response to his own internal necessities. I let a moment or two elapse and then followed him.

We were alone, although it was not impossible that the men's room was bugged. But I had allowed for that in my plan. Still, so as not to seem that I was performing exclusively for the PIDE's benefit, I turned on the taps of the sink—as they do in American films—and addressed my companion.

"Senhor, I am instructed by Dr. Salazar to deliver a package to you for you to take to someone in Lisbon. It is a mission of some delicacy. He relies upon your discretion."

He looked at me—as I assumed he would—with hauteur that was intended to cover his doubts and uncertainties.

"Surely, sir, you are joking."

"Not entirely," I replied. "But that is the story which you may tell the authorities if you are questioned. It will be sufficient to satisfy them."

"And the real story?"

"It is a manuscript," I said. "It is an account of these odd proceedings to which we all have been parties. You gentlemen are protected by your public eminence. I am a mere writer, an obscure poet and journalist. I have no such protection but may be, I fear, disposable, once our masters have finished with me."

"I can understand your concern," he said. "What I don't understand is how you presume to involve me in your machinations!"

"I am, sir, an admirer of yours. Accordingly, I am offering you a way of not being involved. I am offering to keep you out of these . . . machinations, as you call them."

"I don't understand," he said. He was impatient but still curious and worried. Menace, after all, was everywhere and

anywhere, even in the schemes of an utterly insignificant journalist and poet.

"My account of these goings-on is designed to embarrass the
government. It is a kind of insurance policy for me. If I should
somehow disappear, my instructions are that the manuscript is
to be published. The best way for the new regime to keep its
secret, then, is to keep me alive, so that I may continue to send
messages out, instructions that the manuscript remain un-
opened and unread."

"I see. And my role in this?"

"Will be simple and anonymous. But if you refuse me, then
I'll have to turn to one of the others. Or perhaps I have already
done so. Perhaps there are several copies of the manuscript.
And in any one of them I could name the man who has refused
to help me so that he appears to be my accomplice. I've kept
you out of it so far, and I dislike having to threaten, but you see
how it is. You could become a minor literary figure, not just in
the comedy going on in the next room but in some PIDE
slapstick in an Aljube dungeon. You understand, sir, that I
regret having to behave so badly, but I am forced to protect
myself. I am under compulsion—as all of us seem to be."

"I deliver your small package?" he asked. "That's all?"

"And if you are caught, you can tell them I told you it was
on instructions from Dr. Salazar."

"I'll let you know," he promised. "We'll talk at the next
meeting."

"I'll have the package ready for you."

"But . . . what is to prevent me from turning to them now?"
he asked.

"I'd tell them that you have already done me this service and
then developed cold feet. They won't know whether to believe
you or me, of course, but the safer course will be to assume that
I have managed to get a copy of my manuscript out into the
world. My guess is that I shall bear up better under their
inquisition than you, because you will be innocent and the
outrage will therefore be all the greater for you. As the guilty
party, I shall be better resigned. Do you want to test out my
theory?"

"You are a terrible person, a presumptuous and irresponsible person!"

"And you, sir? I don't think anyone in this building can afford to indulge in name-calling or insults," I said. "It would be better if, in a spirit of comradeship, we acknowledged our brotherhood in suffering and desperation."

"Shit!" he exclaimed. Or perhaps he meant it as an epithet for me.

My maneuver seems to have worked. My worst fear was that he'd come out of the men's room, immediately announce to the meeting that I was a traitor and a fool, and have me arrested there on the spot. But no such thing happened.

My next worry was that, upon reflection, he might see some move I'd failed to defend against, that he might devise a way of turning me in that evening or the next day without endangering himself or jeopardizing the position of the Caetano government.

But nothing happened. There were no footsteps in the corridor, nor, after I managed to fall asleep, any sudden flood of lights as they came to drag me away. I had prepared a copy of this manuscript. I had contrived a relatively compact package. And I had addressed it.

All that now remains is for me to hand it over to my courier.

I suppose he might turn it over to them.

But they won't know whether or not I was telling the truth about the other copy. It would make sense to have done this twice, wouldn't it? Each as a check and protection for the other!

Some cynic might suppose that it wasn't necessary for me to smuggle out even the one copy. That intricate and squalid mind might congratulate himself on having had the insight to divine that the mere claim to have done so is a threat—in a single manuscript that I have retained here in the palace where, presumably, it would be found if my room and belongings were searched.

Yes, well, that's possible. But can you rely on it, my not-so-good man? Can you absolutely depend on the cowardice of a poet, knowing for a certainty that none of these worthies would have been susceptible to the threats and persuasions I have described in the foregoing?

I dare you!

If you're wrong, we may be cell mates, which would be an elegant kind of punishment for us both. For having thus under-estimated each other.

Think about it!

II

Salazar Blinks Twice

◆

1

IT WAS IN HIS BRIEFCASE, just as the journalist had said it would be. The package was addressed to Srta. Sidonia de Castro. Rinaldo Gomes, Minister of Trade in the Salazar government, stared at its brown wrapper for a moment, felt the weight of the object in his hands, and then quickly thrust it back into the depths of his case.

His driver, he had no doubt, was PIDE.

And he was tempted, right there, to turn the manuscript over to the driver and be done with it.

He was afraid not to do that, but he was also afraid to do it— as the journalist had known he'd be.

He had got this far and would almost certainly be able to continue with it to the door of his house where the driver would stop, get out, and hold the door open for him, as if he were only a chauffeur and Gomes were still an important person, a Cabinet minister, a man to whom such courtesies were merely normal perquisites.

But then he'd be committed. As no doubt he already was. His instincts were to wait and take the time to analyze the situation. He wanted the time to think out what his next move ought to be. He would read the manuscript, first of all, to make sure that it was as dangerous as he supposed. To confirm his fears.

And then he would find out who this Senhorita Sidonia de Castro was. Close to the journalist. His sister, perhaps, or his cousin? Or, more likely, his mistress.

A little time, and Gomes would know enough to understand what his choices were. There was no need to leap just yet. He could fall back upon the story the journalist had given him— that this was an errand he was running for Dr. Salazar. That wouldn't hold up indefinitely, but it would probably serve to get him through the risks of the moment.

Sufficient to the moment are the risks thereof.

As the large, comfortable limousine rolled through the streets of Lisbon, Gomes tried not to let himself be too much lulled by the ostentatious comfort of the big car. It was like being back in the Ministry again.

It was like that, but it wasn't that. A slight but enormous difference.

One was real and the other an illusion. One was permanent and the other ephemeral.

On the other hand, as his own wife had pointed out to him, it is only the cheap things and the ephemeral pleasures that we truly own. The others are only momentarily ours and they have a life of their own, passing from our possession to that of others, our children or our debtors, or other rich and grasping people who are misguided enough to believe that they can claim the loyalty of these expensive and inert and fatally fickle objects. Houses, cars, jewels, pieces of good furniture . . . They migrate as mysteriously as the birds in the air and the fish in the sea, obedient to their own laws, following their own instincts.

Luisa, his wife, was given to saying outrageous things like that. It was sometimes charming. But, more often than not, distressing.

Gomes would have been upset but not outraged if he had made some mistake, if the hopelessness of his situation were the result of some blunder or miscalculation on his part. There would be a reasonableness, a justice, however harsh, and even a kind of comfort in knowing that in some remote way, he had deserved this relegation to the shadow cabinet.

That was what they called the leaders of the opposition party in England—the shadow cabinet. Here, of course, there was no opposition.

But there were shadows. As in Plato's cave. Flickering doubles, projections of reality without substance or weight.

He was inconsequential. Powerless and valueless.

He was one of those cheap and ephemeral diversions to which Luisa was so sentimentally attracted.

Insufferable!

The PIDE man played out his little charade, holding the door open for Gomes and pretending to be a driver. It was catching, Gomes decided, this business of imposture and pretense. Like one of those influenza epidemics.

That word, in the original Italian, was *influenza del diavolo*—the devil's influence.

Easy enough, perhaps, to equate Salazar with the Prince of Darkness, Gomes reflected. The hard part was associating Caetano with the Heavenly Host.

His gate having clanged shut behind him, Gomes heard the soothing sound of the car's muffled purr as the PIDE man headed back to the garage on his way to headquarters and the filing of his report.

So far, so good. Gomes would read the manuscript and then decide what to do—perhaps turn it over to this Senhorita de Castro or possibly send it, himself, to publishers in Paris and London and Madrid and Milan.

None of whom would be interested. In Portuguese politics? It is at best a cultivated taste.

But in Brazil . . .?

Where the nuts come from!

Unless the journalist was PIDE also. And this entire exercise was a test?

In which case, Gomes realized he had failed. The correct

thing would have been to turn the package over immediately to the PIDE driver.

Perhaps they had all been tested in this way?

Would he be the only failure? Or could he rely on the duplicity and cowardice of every one of his colleagues?

Most of them, surely, but all?

But perhaps a simple majority would be enough. A kind of vote, Gomes decided. Almost democratic.

Very funny!

He put the attaché case in his study and locked it. He usually kept his papers under lock and key, as if there were information on matters of state in them. As if there were real secrets.

The only secret was the one he kept from Luisa—that he was a part of a childish game that was being played on the old man.

If Luisa suspected what it was he did with his time, she would . . . He could hardly imagine it.

She would laugh.

And her laughter would unman him.

He would be destroyed in his own home, overthrown and reduced to a kind of lapdog. He would be without force and power.

The laughter would carry from the study and the living room, through to the other rooms of the house, including, of course, the bedroom.

A man cannot make love to a woman who is laughing at him. It is a physical impossibility. His virile force deserts him. He is rudely ejected from the domain of her body and is thrust out—as any impostor deserves to be thrust out.

He could feel his penis shrivel at the mere thought of it.

The respect a man should have at home comes from what he is able to impose on the outside or to extract from his peers in a grudging world. Without that respect, the wife is sure to rebel. To be, sooner or later, unfaithful? Why not? What would be the point of fidelity to a clown, or loyalty to a pitiable figure the woman can no longer admire?

The silvery peals of her laughter, were like knives glinting in the air. He could feel them as well as hear them.

They cut him to the heart, to the soul.

It was not merely the random choice of that damned cur of a journalist that had selected him for this torment. Gomes had no doubt but that the journalist, too, was an instrument of fate. It was Gomes's agony! The trial of his spirit! He insisted at least on the dignity of his suffering. He might be a supernumerary in the government's episodic skit that they were staging for Salazar's benefit, but here he was the leading player. This was his punishment for his complicity in that other business.

And Luisa, his dear Luisa, was the instrument of his torture, selected by the all-seeing and all-powerful gods for the exquisite torments to which only she could subject him.

Salazar had no such vulnerability. He'd never risked it. Or, as Gomes pondered the question, perhaps Salazar hadn't needed it. Sex, companionship, domination . . . If one had a country, what did one need with a woman?

But Mussolini had what's-her-name!

On the other hand, as Mussolini found out, Italy is a whore, faithless, heartless, and utterly incapable of any further degradation.

Hitler, though, had Eva Braun.

But only because he supposed he was entitled to such services and perquisites.

Lenin and Krupskaya?

Oh, no!

He began to laugh. It was outrageous and wonderful, hysterically funny. He roared with laughter. Luisa heard him and came in to ask if he were all right.

"Oh, yes. I'm fine," he said. "It's just that something struck me as very funny."

"A state secret, I suppose?" she asked, teasingly.

"Actually, it is," he said.

◆

What he could not figure out, though, was whether the prankster who had imposed this joke on Portugal was somebody in the PIDE or someone higher up.

Caetano?

God? Answering too late the prayers of his devoted Cardinal Patriarch Cerejeira?

He looked it up. And, yes, it was just as he'd thought. Lenin, too, had been so stricken. Unable to speak. And for years he had lain there, blinking and twitching, as Krupskaya interpreted his thoughts.

Or made them up and attributed them to her speechless spouse.

What she wrote down and said had come from her husband was *Lenin's Testament,* one of the main burdens of which was that, under no circumstances, should Comrade Stalin be entrusted with power. According to Lenin, Stalin was untrustworthy, ill-mannered, had a funny Georgian accent and terrible table manners. And he should be got rid of as quickly as possible.

True? Not true?

It was perfectly possible that this was an insulting story told to schoolchildren in Western Europe, or anyway in Portugal, to teach them contempt for the Communists. Maybe Salazar even invented it!

And here he was, living it out.

Along with his whole cabinet!

According to that story, Stalin called Krupskaya into his office and gave her hell, warning her that there was only one Lenin, but there could be any number of widows. She could be replaced. And would be, unless she shut her big mouth.

From now on, pronouncements she attributed to Lenin would be cleared in advance.

And she agreed, of course.

Or maybe not. Maybe there was another Krupskaya. Maybe there were as many Krupskayas as there are Santa Clauses on the streets of New York at Christmas.

The faith of the little children is remarkable!

And now, like Lenin, Salazar lies sputtering and twitching and blinking, and a woman interprets for him, and the world manages to spin itself through its proper orbit.

Luisa came to tell him that lunch would be ready soon. She looked at him, inquiringly.

He had been laughing before and now he was sober and sad. And he knew she was puzzled and could not explain his sadness any more than he had been able to explain his laughter.

2

LATE THAT NIGHT, Gomes read the manuscript. His wife was upstairs in bed, almost certainly asleep. The entire house was asleep, not silent but in that fitful manner of city dwellings, with intriguing and sometimes disturbing creaks and rumblings. It was, Gomes knew, only a trick of the imagination, and yet when the refrigerator in the kitchen switched its motor on, the whole building seemed to startle.

In his study, at the edge of the pool of light his lamp spread on the tooled Florentine leather of his desktop, Gomes felt something akin to the fears and fancies of his boyhood, the conviction that there were savage beasts lurking in the dark places in his nursery, bears and huge dogs and even crocodiles, lost, frenzied with hunger, and at any moment about to strike.

Those old worries were almost welcome, companions of such long standing, nearly friends by now. And compared to the real worries and fears he had learned to live with, they were less menacing than they had been four decades ago. There was still the possibility of attack from some unexpected quarter, Gomes knew, and the likeliest eventuality was that the manuscript on the desk before him would come to life, pounce, and bite him in the throat.

It was not the invention of the PIDE, however. Of that he was all but certain.

They are clever enough, those bastards. But they don't have the requisite lightness, the sense of humor. What they can't do is be funny about their work.

It wasn't a Portuguese failing, Gomes thought, but a more general defect of that profession, no matter where they practiced. The CIA, or the KGB, or Savak, or Mossad, or the British or French secret services . . . they all shared an earnestness that could not tolerate satire, let alone contrive, for whatever purpose, such an exercise in self-parody.

So he was real, this journalist and poet. Soi-disant, at any rate. Or maybe he was an actual poet, even perhaps a good one.

That would be funniest of all.

What Portugal does to her sons is figured in what she does to her cork trees—their twists and contortions suggesting the agonies of religious and political experience.

But Gomes had enough to worry about on his own account. This poet seemed to be able to take care of himself well enough. To hell with him.

Luisa lay in bed, lightly snoring—which pleased Gomes. She was almost girlish this way, or at least less formidable.

She should have been a man. Her father, the admiral, would have been happier. And Luisa, without that little feminizing vowel at the end of her name, would have been more comfortable, having more scope for her managerial skills and better occasion to test her mettle. As a politician's wife, she could give little dinner parties and go to luncheons, but there was something odd about her dedication to these activities, as though she were using a military sword to spread pâté.

Poor Luisa! All she had to work with was her sleek and rather unsatisfactory husband. Who was not enterprising enough. Not bold enough or ruthless enough.

And, mostly, Gomes profoundly believed, not lucky enough.

She looked sweet, poignantly appealing as she lay there with those moist sputterings occasionally erupting from the gentle rise and fall of her pretty chest. Gomes thought of sex.

But that would involve waking her.

If only one could devise a way of fucking them while they were asleep.

He thought of that as he undressed and got into his plum-colored silk pajamas from a very expensive haberdasher in London. Would that not amount to another form of what the journalist had called Salazarismo?

As he was lying in bed, waiting for sleep to come, it occurred to him that there was another possible move he ought to consider. The members of the Salazar government met informally, not to lobby for one position or another about pending business—there wasn't any business anymore—but simply to lend some plausibility to their routines and fill in the empty spaces that yawned so rudely in their daybooks and pocket calendars.

They might act together on a matter of this seriousness, one in which each of them was so intimately touched.

Of course, that meant they had to trust one another. Which would be something of a novelty—as Salazar had recently demonstrated so vividly, making them swear that oath of mutual loyalty.

Still, might there not be one or two he could confide in? A faction? Were there not even two men of honor in what had once been the government of Portugal?

We are born alone and we die alone. And we conduct our business affairs and run our governments in a torment of loneliness and yearning.

Like babies, longing for the breast.

He reached out for Luisa's breast, small but well shaped and reliably comforting.

Best of all, he did not have to wake her. She adjusted herself in her sleep.

Gomes was pleased with himself. Perhaps that was St. Joseph's trick—and more than sufficient reason for his sainthood. The old fox, for whom most people felt some mixture of sympathy and contempt, hadn't been cuckold to the Holy

Ghost after all. He'd managed to achieve what other and lesser men had merely dreamt of.

And Mary still thought she was a virgin!

Gomes awoke with a conviction that he was doing the right thing. The prudent thing, at any rate. He had looked at the manuscript. What remained now was for him to scrutinize the recipient. And he had all the leisure a man could want. The terrible problem of finding things to do that would keep him busy and away from the house was, at least for the time being, resolved. Or absorbed into the larger problem of avoiding the catastrophe that seemed everywhere to be looming.

He bathed, shaved, dressed, and broke his fast. Then he drove off toward the residence of the journalist's addressee. She lived up near the citadel in one of those areas that had not been much affected by the periodic earthquakes that have served to make Lisbon one of Europe's more modern and attractive cities. The winding streets and the old-fashioned buildings were chic now only because they were small and dark and uncomfortable. But what is a little discomfort if one has servants to cope with it, after all?

He parked his car, wandered about in the neighborhood a bit, and stopped for a cup of coffee in a café down the street from Senhorita de Castro's building. He wasn't quite sure what he hoped to learn in this way, but it was a pleasant morning, still fresh but with the season's warmth beginning to assert itself. One didn't want strenuous exertion on a day like this, but sitting at a café table and sipping coffee was within one's modest capabilities.

You have to trust in the generosity of the gods a little, Gomes had always believed, if they are to be given a chance to show that generosity. Or, putting it another way, you have to be sitting down in order for their prizes to fall into your lap.

He looked up at the pattern made by the branches of a plane tree against a stuccoed wall. A small delight, for which young women with sketch pads know how to be grateful. And when he looked down again, he saw the postman approaching.

Yes, of course!

He finished his coffee, got up, sauntered over toward the postman, and opened his wallet displaying his impressive ministerial credential.

"I need to take a brief glance at some return addresses on some of the envelopes in your care," he explained.

The postman held forth his pouch. Gomes sorted through the mail until he found the letters for de Castro. And from de Castro? Her family was from Évora in Alto Alentejo. Now it would be a simple matter to identify her father and mother, from which Gomes could guess something about the daughter's political predilections. Or certainly her political weight.

"You will say nothing of this," he warned.

"No, sir."

"Excellent!"

"No, Excellence!" the postman said, as if Gomes had been correcting him.

Part of the odd arrangement Gomes had with the government —the real government, that is—gave him the use of one of the vacant desks at the Ministry from noon until two o'clock, when most of the regular staff were out having lunch. There was a small cubicle off one of the back rooms in which one drawer of the small steel desk was reserved for his use. And he who had once been the *capitão* was now reduced to this. For a certain sort of temper, what delight! As of course, Gomes understood perfectly well. It was bitter medicine indeed for him to exercise this prerogative and take advantage of the facilities available to him. Along with the desk there was also a box for his mail, not that much mail ever appeared anymore.

Still, he had retained some friends among the clerical staff, people who remembered him when he'd been an important person, some of whom were grateful for favors he'd once done them. Some just felt sorry for one who had fallen from such a height to abysmal ridiculousness.

One of these was a young man named Manuel who was at least well mannered enough to keep his motives to himself, whatever they were. He was, at any rate, an obliging fellow. He

had a distracting mustache, all dark, almost black, but with a
blaze of white on the left-hand side, about a third of the way
over. One tried not to stare at this blaze. Manuel was in charge
of interdepartmental inquiries and was a useful person to know.
Back in the old days, this would have been an appropriate
question for him to handle, and Gomes asked if he might
impose . . .

"But of course," Manuel answered. "It would be no imposi-
tion whatever. I should be pleased to be of any service. What
can I do for you?"

He asked Manuel to find out what he could about the de
Castro family of Évora. Where was their money from? How
much was there? What kinds of power and influence went with
it? It was, he assured Manuel, actually a matter of state. The
prohibitions against making such inquiries for purely personal
motives would in no way be violated, he promised.

"Consider it done," Manuel assured him.

"Obrigado!"

A long, leisurely lunch of smoked ham and melon, spider
crab, and *toucinho do céu,* our honey-and-almond confection,
and it was almost time for Gomes to return home. He browsed
the fashionable shops in the Rossio not so much because he
wanted to buy anything as to be able to congratulate himself on
his self-restraint.

Patience, patience. That is what separates the men from the
boys, the sheep from the goats, and the wheat from the chaff.
Slow and steady wins the race.

His head was full of that kind of used furniture. It's what all
such people believe, what they have to believe so that they can
hope to succeed where their betters have failed. These are
their consolations in time of trouble, and the pieties with
which they give thanks for the occasional glints of good fortune
that randomly illuminate their lives. They don't even dare
acknowledge their own luck, which is unreliable, but prefer to
credit their dull stolidity, which will never desert them and
can never fail.

Poor Gomes!

I am imagining him, of course. But the PIDE can't be quite sure, can they? They know I've changed his name and have taken liberties, but they are not so stupid as never to have heard of the roman à clef.

Who is Gomes?

Or, rather, which one of that cowardly pack of puppets and clowns is Gomes?

And who is this Senhorita de Castro?

Does her father have extensive land holdings outside of Évora with cork trees and wine grapes burgeoning beneath the beneficent rays of the life-giving sun? Is he the last scion of a noble house whose daughter, rich and indulged, has fled the stifling protections of life in the upper classes of Portuguese society to drink of the heady liquors (and smoke and swallow the even headier substances available in Paris and Rome, Taormina and Mykonos)?

Intelligent but headstrong!

Gorgeous but proud and, as some would say, spoiled!

Compared to her, Luisa Gomes is a pussycat!

And poor Gomes finds that his fate is in her attractive, well-manicured, but somewhat fidgety hands?

Outrageous!

Outrage upon outrage, a bruise upon a bruise!

But exactly what he deserves. Such plodding earnestness cries out for chastisement. Especially when it presumes to assert itself as a virtue.

All that is needed is that the PIDE believe in the possibility of what I've either invented or reported (albeit with some embellishment).

Their attempts at fiction—for Salazar, or for the public at large—ought to make them more vulnerable to the fictions and inventions of others.

I'll find out, soon enough.

Meanwhile, Dona Maria has asked me to report accurately what news I can of the Caetano government so that Salazar can better prepare himself for his next moves.

She said this with a perfectly straight face. "His next moves."

Sic.

Sick!

The point is that he can't move. Can't do much more than swallow and breathe and, with real effort, blink.

Once for yes, twice for no.

And he wants to consider his moves? Perhaps he might decide to fly like a big bird over the Tagus, looking down at the glinting of the Salazar Bridge, soaring, banking, swooping, and diving, astonishing them all with his grace and supernatural power.

3

FROM THE FIRST MOMENT HE SAW HER, he was transfixed, amazed that there could be a creature of such perfection wandering carelessly about the streets . . . not of Lisbon, necessarily, but anywhere on earth. Such pride, such ease, such assurance, and such innate chic. He noticed the way her hair bounced ever so saucily with the rhythm of her gait. He remarked on the tone of her suntan that was set off by the white linen to which she was partial. He took in the good shoes and handbag, the gold necklace, the Hermès scarf she wore loosely at her neck, and all these things seemed to make sense, to have been foreordained in order to complement her exact kind of beauty.

Longing, and then, immediately, jealousy. Because she was that journalist's woman.

Or had been?

Or had merely allowed that poor creature to dream of her, abject and desperate.

And yet, and yet . . . He knew how it was with some of these women, how their heads are easily turned by the smooth palaver of lightweight litterateurs.

He was in the café again, sitting where he had been patiently stationed for several days now, watching for the woman who would fit the description (accurate but how inadequate) he had put together from the security folder to which Manuel had managed to gain access.

He was almost happy to have an excuse to speak to her, some business—however desperate and preposterous—to transact. After all, what could she do to him that she had not already done?

She had his life in her hands, the lives of all of them for that matter.

And yet beautiful women do that, are accustomed to doing that. They assume, as they walk down the boulevard, enjoying the morning's freshness, that the spring in their step comes from the hearts of strangers that have been flung down before them like so many velvet cloaks.

It is how they've been walking for years.

And for a cautious fellow like Gomes, it was almost a relief to have his destiny yanked from him, to be light-headedly careless of what happened to him. Not that this was much different from the powerlessness he felt in the face of the Caetano government and, more particularly, under the watchful eyes of the PIDE. But just as there are religious experiences that need personification in the physical remains of some martyr or saint, so there are philosophical situations that need a humane leavening, an embodiment of the kind one finds in the presence of an adored woman.

Luisa had been such a woman for Gomes once, impossibly remote and unspeakably desirable. But she had lost some of her allure simply by her having condescended to marry him. As Wagner understood full well, making Brünnhilde lose her immortality before she could marry Siegfried.

Gomes had no expectations that his outcome would be any better than Siegfried's, but he supposed he was fortunate to have had two such experiences in one lifetime.

Not that this amounted, quite yet, to an actual experience. He had not actually addressed her so far, had not yet imposed himself upon her consciousness.

A godly feeling, though, to know something about her life that she did not know—that she would be meeting one desperate man who was bearing a manuscript that was a message from another man, just as desperate. That their actions and reactions would be casting huge and distorted shadows on the landscape of their country. Or that the great love of her life, brief but perfect, was about to begin.

Gomes was not absolutely certain of the third of these propositions, but to conjoin it with the first two gave it some appearance of substance. And, as long as he was doing no more than sitting in a café and fantasizing, why not let the fantasies be agreeable ones? The whims of the fates would make themselves manifest soon enough, fulfilling or dashing his dreams. Or, just as likely, modifying them into some grotesque parody, as if in reprimand.

He was enjoying himself. He was also afraid. Once he'd delivered the manuscript, he had no doubt but that she'd read it, no matter what the instructions were from the journalist. Any journalist who expects a woman to keep a manuscript and not look at it is crazy or stupid, doesn't know anything about human nature, and is in the wrong business.

Gomes had no such hopes or illusions. As far as he was concerned, she'd read it. And then she would be the mistress of all their destinies. His, the journalist's, and those of the other men of the cabinet. Even that of Salazar himself.

Fate. *Fado!* The other great Portuguese product, along with cork, sardines, tungsten, olives, and wine. The sad songs of the cabaret singers about the grinding down of all valor and beauty and aspiration into the dust. The heritage of the gypsies and the moors, but all the more precious for that. And painful, but all the more intimate for that, like a sore place one touches again and again to find that, yes, it is still tender.

But at least the feeling is not yet gone. And life has not yet left us.

Fado!

A dark lady is often the subject of such songs. Or if not, then their singer.

A lady much like the Senhorita de Castro. To whom, sooner or later, Gomes would have to make his address. Saying something quite true and yet quite conventional, like "Forgive me,

Senhorita, but I must speak with you for you hold my life in your hand. . . ."

The last tattered remnant of the traditions of gallantry and courtly love.

So much the better, Gomes decided.

An intelligent, sensitive man, a man who was in fact a connoisseur of sensibility, Gomes knew that this was the best part, this time before the moment of action and commitment. Here one could adjust, speculate, telescope time or endlessly extrude it, revising as a painter adds a subtle touch here or a bold daub there, to get just the right balance of tension and repose, energy and tranquil reflection. Once he rose from the chair and approached her, there would be no going back and he would have descended to the crude plane of the boulevard on which any banal *flâneur* could rub elbows with him or jostle her.

And yet, not to commit the matter to the tests of the external world and the arbitration of time and the fates would be cowardly. Self-indulgent. And a little précieux?

That, too.

So, after a brandy for celebration and maybe one more for courage (he called it luck, I have no doubt), he arose and approached her.

No question but it was she. And the fellow behind her was not altogether a stranger, either, for that matter.

Gomes walked right on by, looking neither to the left nor the right. He might have been blind or homosexual. Or a religious. He seemed to any passerby almost too oblivious of such an attractive woman.

But that not-quite-familiar man, wasn't he PIDE?

Better to wait, to play it safe. Another time would serve as well as this. And there was no sense in compromising the young lady.

He felt very shrewd, having noticed that face.

Although, now that he looked around, he could not be so sure.

At any rate, it was too late, she had disappeared around a corner.

He could never catch up. Not without running. And he did not want to recite his opening lines while struggling to catch his breath.

Another day, then.

At home, he was convinced that he had been correct. The man was PIDE. And the report was on the appropriate desk already. That Gomes had failed to make the contact.

That assumed, of course, that the journalist was a plant. And that Senhorita de Castro was also a party to their intricate operation.

What sense did any of this make? Very little, except in an emotional way. Gomes was convinced that somewhere in some obscure office, younger, lesser men were laughing at him, knew what he was doing—at every moment of the day and night— and were braying in scornful polyphony.

Damn them!

"Are you coming to bed?" Luisa asked, mildly annoyed.

"I have work to do," he responded.

"In here?"

"I'll go to my study," he told her.

"Thank you," she said, rather coldly.

And if they knew about this exchange, as they probably did, they'd be laughing all the harder.

He looked about for the telltale signs of their hidden microphones. But he knew he didn't know enough to be able to spot such things.

He couldn't ask Manuel, his friend in the Ministry, either. Not this kind of question.

How long, O Lord!

At the next cabinet meeting, I left a message on Gomes's pad: "W.C., S.V.P., A.S.A.P."

He puzzled it out. And eventually, he took himself off to the men's room. I followed.

"Well? Have you delivered it?"

"The time has not been propitious."

"You're joking!"

"I've tried. I have tried."

"You must do better. Or I shall tell them that you are my confederate, that you have been holding the manuscript for me. They will search your house. And they will find it and you'll be off to some copra plantation by tomorrow afternoon!"

"And you? What do you think will happen to you?" he asked, showing a little spirit.

"I agree. We'll both fall. I'm already at the bottom of the pit, though, and don't have much to fear. You are up in the branches of a fairly tall tree, with a certain degree of freedom and comfort, picking the fruit and enjoying the view. You have more to fear than I do from the same disaster. You have much more to lose."

"I will deliver it," he said.

"Good. And if you try to deceive me, I'll know. I've worked it out. The only safe thing for you to do is deal honestly with me. Believe me! Any other course, no matter how tempting, will bring ruin on you and your family."

"Of course, that could be an empty threat," he said, smiling.

"It could be. You want to try me?" I offered. I flushed my urinal, zipped, and left before he could answer.

I was bluffing, of course. But I assumed that he would not have the courage to test me. A brave man would have delivered the manuscript. Or would have claimed to have done so. Or would have refused. Or would have defied me and denounced me to the PIDE.

In short, a brave man would have taken any other course but the one Gomes had chosen.

Or, no, that's unfair. Any other course but the one to which Gomes's character had condemned him.

It is possible, considering those by whom Salazar has always been surrounded, to feel sorry for the old man. Look what he has had to work with, to put up with! Imagine the disgust. Imagine the loneliness.

To make a country is difficult enough. To rouse it from its centuries-long slumber is a lifetime's task sufficiently arduous and demanding. But to have to do it with these coxcombs, these commedia dell'arte buffoons!

How demeaning. How humiliating.

Poor Salazar!

4

YOU THINK I'M BEING TOO HARD ON HIM, poor old, silly old, dithery old Gomes?

Hardly. He is not, after all, one of the first rank of Salazar's ghost ministers. He is one of the lesser and younger of a decadent version of what never even started out at any lofty level.

I mean, have you ever heard of any of Portugal's ministers?

Well, sure, it's a setup. I've got my candidate here, the one man among all these gofers and yes-men, these toadies and stooges whose name a reasonably intelligent and well-informed person might have heard mentioned. Not to summon it up in active memory perhaps, but to recognize it passively.

Hint: He was a Minister of External Affairs.

Second hint: He was a physician.

Third and last hint: He actually won the Nobel Prize. For medicine. In 1949. No joke. You can look it up. After all, how many Portuguese have won Nobel Prizes? They don't have a category for carving wooden chickens. Or for cooking shellfish.

And the answer, ladies and gentlemen, *messieurs et mes-dames, senhors e senhoras,* is . . . António Egas Moniz.

You react minimally. Who? What?

António Moniz! Sure, you remember. The man who invented the prefrontal lobotomy! Which is, admittedly, not much in favor anymore. And Dr. Moniz is not so highly thought of perhaps as he once may have been, now that it has been established that his methods were somewhat haphazard and his record-keeping procedures a bit negligent. Still, before the introduction of tranquilizers and other such psychiatric pharmaceuticals, Dr. Moniz and his operation enjoyed some popularity, with the families of his patients, if not with the patients themselves. His American disciple, a Dr. Walter Freeman, refined the procedure and went in transversely in what was called, by the more jocular cutups among neurosurgeons, the ice-pick operation.

And that's the top of the heap, the most distinguished and accomplished of our country's diplomatists and ministers. I mean, this fellow was also an historian, literary critic, and composer. And a gentleman. He was a member of the old nobility and he retired from public life after a political quarrel that led to a duel, which he won. This was in 1919, a little before Salazar's time, but at least he had some style and presence. Some weight.

From that acme, one must descend quite some distance before arriving at the level of the present crew, among whom Rinaldo Gomes is by no means the preeminent figure, either in respect of his native intelligence or of his character and courage.

Which was why I'd picked him out to begin with.

All he had to do was walk away that first time we talked and either turn the manuscript over to his PIDE driver/watchdog or else just burn it, but have the good sense to lie to me about it when I asked him if he'd delivered it yet to Senhorita de Castro.

It is one of the great comforts of my isolation here in the palace to imagine the encounter when it finally took place, the approach and the transfer of the incendiary pages.

Meanwhile, Senhorita de Castro was utterly unaware of the impending adventure that was preparing itself for her, like a thundercloud in the night sky.

Which served her right.

Attractive young women, women of wealth and leisure, ought to devote themselves to something more serious and socially useful than the search for new clothes, new perfumes, new foods, new drinks, and new men to flirt with. They owe it to God and country to try to improve the conditions of poverty and ignorance of so many of their countrymen. Or to promote culture—in however small a way. As, for example, by encouraging the work of young writers, even young poet/journalists they happen to meet at social gatherings.

Unfair? But look at it this way. If a young girl like Beatrice could win a kind of immortality just by attracting the admiring glance of a Florentine poet who happened to notice her on the Lungarno, why should a contemporary Portuguese woman be protected from ridicule—even calumny—for having so brusquely dismissed a poet who was her countryman?

It wasn't even that she disliked my poetry! She'd never seen a line of it, so far as I knew.

It wasn't the poetry she was laughing at, but me. The fact that I weigh a few pounds more than the romantic tradition allows its poets struck her as funny.

Or maybe it was the combination of the expansive waistline and the recessive hairline. . . .

A poet's life is of the mind, of the heart and spirit. What have we to do with diets and gymnasiums?

"You? A poet? You look like a . . . like a druggist. All you need is the little mustache."

And she laughed, a terrible, perfectly delightful laugh that tinkled like little silvery bells.

I can still hear it.

The laughter of the others that chimed in with hers was terrible to endure, but the memory of that has faded. It is the echo of her laugh that has stayed with me all these years.

To whom could I better address the manuscript, then?

Either she will do the right thing and emerge as that benefactress and patriot she should have been, having been summoned to greatness by the chances of her birth and privilege, or else she will be made to pay.

It's up to her. Which is not only fair but a kind of poetic justice.

The best kind!

To be perfectly honest, my arrest was not irrelevant. In better and more usual circumstances, I might have met a dozen other women, some of whom might have been as pretty or as rich or, more to the point, as self-assured and queenly as Sidonia de Castro.

And men are faithless. Poets are, anyway. Or this one is. Her mocking image would have lost its place of honor in the gallery of my mind to some other face, or bust, or full-length portrait that chance would have installed there.

But they came and arrested me. They took me away. The soft wax hardened and her visage took on the inevitability of those on postage stamps and currency.

Sidonia de Castro!

Mistress of my soul! For having laughed at me, disbelieving that I could possibly be a poet.

I tried to forget her.

But how do you try to forget something or someone?

Don't think of the number 16! But just to say that is to think of the number 16, as every smart-assed kid knows.

What was bothersome was that I now had an answer for her contemptuous laughter. She didn't have to take my word for it anymore but could now rely on the official certification of the Portuguese government.

According to the PIDE, I was a poet.

Not only a poet but, in a modest way—I hoped it would continue to be modest—a martyr to poetry.

Some bureaucrat had read my work, closely enough anyway to notice that line about crocodile tears and see it as a possible reference to our African embarrassment. And he had seen my poetry as a possible threat to the regime, serious enough to refer my folder to some superior for a decision and eventual action.

And they came to drag me away and lock me up.

◆

I'd have gone willingly—or less unwillingly, anyway—if I'd been able to suppose that Sidonia de Castro was watching them drag me away.

And feeling sorry for how badly she'd behaved. Her face downcast in chagrin, and her hand at her beautiful bosom . . .

I tried to forget her. And of course I failed.

After that terrible meeting, I sent her a book, just to prove to her that she'd been wrong about me. She never bothered to read it.

Or maybe she read it and hated it?

I'd prefer the latter, actually. But my guess is that she never even looked at it, had no idea who the hell I was, didn't connect the book with the plump guy at the party she'd laughed at.

Maybe she opened it, looked at a page or two, and didn't understand any of it. It is perfectly possible that the most complicated texts she can manage are the fashion notes in *Vogue* and *Elle*.

In which case, my sending her the new manuscript will turn out to be a perfect gesture. This book, too, will be safe with her. She will not find it tempting to violate the warning tucked inside the title page which suggests that, for her own safety, she go no further.

She may not get even that far.

But the PIDE, which is where my real readers are, won't be able to rely on that, will they?

How can they imagine such serenity, such self-confidence? For her indifference and her inattention are such as only those luxuries can foster. If Portugal were as assured as this particular young woman, it would hardly need a security police force like the PIDE.

In which case, I might have no readers at all!

Salazar wants to see me.

Dona Maria has brought word that the old man wishes me to appear before him, which is interesting news.

I asked what he wanted, but she was not forthcoming. Either

I did not deserve explanations or else she has no idea, herself, of what her master has in mind.

Even so, it is something of an honor.

I don't suppose I have anything to fear from Salazar. He is not likely to approve of me but neither is he going to be able to afford to get rid of me. He must work with what he has at hand—which means Dona Maria and me.

He could destroy me, inform the PIDE that I have been injecting offensive nonsense into his news reports to make it clear that they are false. . . .

But that would be cutting off his own nose to spite his face.

If I were he, I should be curious just to meet such a fellow, to try to understand what kind of person had behaved in this unpredictable way.

As, indeed, I am in fact curious to confront him. I've seen him before, naturally, but only from across the room, hidden from view by the presence of all those other functionaries. We have not scrutinized one another, have not actually exchanged greetings.

Dona Maria will be there, too, of course. But he must have pressed her already, as hard as he could, for whatever information she could supply about me. Which could not have been much.

The two of us, Dona Maria and myself, are the only Salazar loyalists left in Portugal.

Unless, in some subtle way, one includes—as the PIDE might decide to do—Rinaldo Gomes and Sidonia de Castro.

5

IT WAS NOT MUCH OF AN INTERVIEW. Call it a viewing rather. I looked at him. He looked at me.

It was a little before ten in the evening. Dona Maria had come for me and led me to Salazar's bedroom—the same room as that in which the cabinet pretends to meet. Or in which the pretend cabinet actually meets. Most of the room was in darkness, but in a pool of light from his bedside lamp, Salazar seemed to float—like a survivor of some sea disaster on a small life raft.

The little old man with his thatch of neatly barbered white hair looked up, either at the wall or at me. It was difficult to tell which. For a time, he said nothing, and I said nothing.

Then his right eye started to twitch.

Dona Maria interpreted this to mean, "He wants to know why you have behaved as you've done. What motive can you have?"

"No motive," I said.

He made a kind of gargling noise.

Dona Maria said, "You are either for him or against him. You were being loyal to him or you were mocking him. He wants to know which way it was."

I didn't know what to say. I didn't think he'd believe the truth, even if I were able to tell it to him.

"Nothing will happen to you. He needs you. You know that!"

"I know," I said.

"He is curious, nevertheless."

"I was just being playful. It seemed right at the time. What we're all involved with here is a kind of joke, isn't it? And when you are in the presence of a joke, you joke back. I do. Or I try to. That's all it was."

He considered that for a while. Or, for all I know, he just lay there like a turnip while Dona Maria considered my answer. His eye twitched again, stopped, started again, and stopped.

Dona Maria said, "That is satisfactory. He believes you."

"Is that all?" I asked.

"Yes," she said. "But there is one more question he'd like you to answer. If you can."

"Yes?"

"Is Pais still in office?"

"I don't know. I assume so, but I've no idea."

"Find out, if you can."

"I'll try."

"He thanks you."

"It's all right," I said. "It's the least I owe him."

Sure, there were all kinds of ironies and qualifications, private jokes and mordancies that went along with it, but in some peculiar way I had meant it. I did owe him. The difference between the Aljube Prison and the São Bento Palace is considerable. The food is better. The views are more pleasant. The gardens are attractive. There are no rats or hideous cries in the night.

One could argue that these differences are illusory and that from the proper perspective they are one and the same, or even that the São Bento Palace is the worse place, being the cause of the other, its reason and its source.

Still, as long as I had any choice in the matter, any slight power to influence my fate, I preferred to be in the palace.

◆

Pais was Major Silva Pais, the director of the Policia Internacional e de Defesa do Estado. The PIDE.

Pais is not an uncommon name. It means region or country. As any mad medievalist or absurd modernist might have dreamt up and then rejected because it was so silly and excessive.

Dangerous business, of course. It occurred to me as I lay in my bed and waited for sleep to come that I might be asking for all kinds of trouble. It would be better to keep away from such matters.

I could simply let Salazar know that I hadn't been able to find out anything about Major Pais.

I had no idea whether he was still running the PIDE or was now its prisoner, or was alive or dead.

Nor did I care very much.

A man much feared, but not in himself important. Take away Pais and there is another man in the same uniform behind the same desk.

The style of the tortures may vary a little, but none is gentle or humane.

And the results are boringly the same. The prisoner breaks, gives the names, and sinks into that oblivion which is no longer a punishment but now a reward for which he has yearned.

In a minor way, I was a victim of Pais, but I didn't really give much of a damn about what had happened to him.

But Salazar did.

He cared enough to risk a great deal, letting me come to see him, making me a kind of confidant. Just to find out why I had been broadcasting nonsense? No, I didn't believe that. I couldn't believe that he did anything out of mere curiosity.

He wanted to know about Pais. That was important to him. For some good and practical reason.

I wondered what that could be.

And I realized that out of mere curiosity, I might even make some cautious moves to find out the answer to Salazar's question. Just to see what the old fox would do.

◈

Was it not likely that, having been snared by my nets and having been further entangled by Sidonia's arrogant charms, poor Gomes would be only too happy to run these little errands for me, taking whatever troubles he could to protect himself (and therefore myself, and therefore Salazar) just as a good little errand boy ought to do?

The prospect was indeed pleasing.

I wondered whether Salazar took the same aesthetic pleasure in the mechanisms of statecraft. Back then, when he was actually running the government, or now, lying immobile in his adjustable hospital-issue bed?

I wondered whether the aesthetic consideration varied inversely with the amount of real power. It is a formulation so neat as to be seductive.

But as Einstein asked, would God play at dice with the universe? Neatness can just as easily be a sign of the likelihood of truth.

Feeling better than I had any right to, I fell asleep with the same intellectual liveliness and curiosity as that of a small boy who has heard another chapter of a continuing bedtime story. The pleasure is a complicated one, made up in part of the information he has just acquired, in part of the activity of free-ranging fantasy, his variations and embellishments on the possibilities that have been presented to him, and in part of the assurance that tomorrow evening there will be a correction, an adjustment, and a new opportunity for his flights of fancy.

Are there any joys adult life has to offer that can compare with these?

No, nothing is so easy.

How did I know that Sidonia was even in Lisbon? It was perfectly possible that she was lolling on some beach on the Riviera. Or somewhere even trendier. The Costa Smeralda, say, where the Aga Khan had opened a new resort! Or that was what I'd read in the newspapers.

It was tempting to suppose that this report was false. Religious leaders have no business opening new tourist meccas—if it is not tasteless to use such a phrase in this connection. What proof is there of these ridiculous reports and silly claims? How do we know that, in each capital of Europe, in each major city where the news services maintain offices, there isn't someone like me, sitting at an unimpressive desk and beating his brains to try to come up with another astonishing and amazing fabrication, some simulacrum of a news report that will, by its very boldness, have some drastic effect.

Any effect.

Or, no, not sitting at a desk, but held captive, as I am.

The lucky bastard who has this job on the Costa Smeralda, even if he is chained to the floor in one of the Aga Khan's cabanas, can still look at the fashionable women stretched on their chaises along the apron of the pool, most of them topless, sunning themselves like so many languorous jungle cats.

And Sidonia, her limbs burnished by the suntan oil, her breasts only slightly paler than the rest of her, is by far the loveliest of them all.

The truth of the matter is that I am jealous of Gomes. He may be in for a humiliation, which is what I'd planned and would still bet on, but at least his experience will be real, which is preferable to the insubstantial fantasies to which I am condemned here in the palace.

I have become a citizen of Salazar's imaginary republic, a denizen of the dream world of which he is now the real ruler.

There is some hope, I suppose, in those gargling noises. He is vocalizing, however obscurely. Not inconceivably, he could regain the power of speech.

And then?

Caetano and his henchmen tremble. For real. And they must be humiliated, must avoid one another's eyes with the same genteel studiousness that obtains here in the palace in Salazar's bedroom, when the shadow cabinet meets.

Dishonor on both sides and to all parties!

The police and the army go out on maneuvers and the trains run and the planes take off, but the entire structure quakes when the old man in that bedroom goes: "Gaaah. Gaaah."

Or "Ga-ga!"

The likelihood of my ever being able to exercise as much power as this stricken and speechless old man still retains is very remote.

But then, I never had any such ambitions. The métier of the poet is one that operates on another plane entirely. What troubles me is that I'd always supposed myself to be a creature of the imagination—but I thought it was my own imagination.

It turns out to be his. Which is one more piece of cheap irony. Or, as we say, poetic justice.

The strength of that phrase, though, comes not from the poets but from the gods—whose tastes for humiliations and abrupt reversals are even more refined than our own. Those gods have been dabbling in the destiny business for thousands of years. Their palates are jaded by the ordinary peasant cuisine, and like bored diners, they search for new spices of subtleties and complications that must be beyond most mortal imaginations.

A high-flown metaphor, but characteristic of our national heritage, I dare say. Exactly the kind of thing Camões would have thrown into Os Lusiadas if he could have conformed it to his complicated rhyme scheme.

O Rinaldo! What pratfalls and disasters have those gods in store for you that are better and worse than anything I could have devised?

Will you tell me? If only to blame me for the mess I've managed to get you into?

I count on that!

6

AND WHAT DID HE DO, our paragon, our model of suave chivalry, our beloved Rinaldo?

Having sat there at the café table long enough for Sidonia to notice him noticing her, long enough for her to have begun to worry lest he be some sort of nuisance, a masher or molester, the kind of sordid pest that is the stock-in-trade of cautious fathers and producers of horror films, he made his move. He approached her, looming up from the plaza like a roused beast and bearing down on her. Crazed, she thought, and dangerous, even here in a public place where she could cry out for help.

As she intended to do. Her mouth was actually open and she could feel the muscles working at the base of her tongue. But before she could get that first piercing scream delivered into the air, he addressed her by name.

"Senhorita! Senhorita de Castro!"

She hesitated, still feeling the impulse to flee or to cry out but caught by the social conventions at least long enough to allow him one more sentence.

"Take this, please. It is from Carlos. The poet. Your friend."

"I know no Carlos."

"Please! For pity's sake. Take it. It's a manuscript."

"I know no poets."

"My life is in your hands! For God's sake, Senhorita!"

"Leave me alone. Go away or I'll scream. I'll call the police!"

"You can't!"

She turned away, about to run, but he reached out and caught her by the sleeve of her coat. He thrust the package into her hands and then turned and fled himself, running away from her and looking from the diminishing rear no longer threatening but ridiculous, rather like a small boy who has performed some ritual prank—putting the bag of dogshit on the doorstep, ringing the doorbell, and setting the bag alight, so that the householder must react by stamping out the flames and getting the shit on his shoe.

The bolder boys jeer from across the street.

The cowards content themselves with imagining the scene.

As Rinaldo Gomes did, too.

And how do I know this? On what authority do I speak?

You think you've found me out, eh? I'm up to my old tricks again, supposing things and asserting them to be actual, when obviously I could not have been there.

But I have my sources. As will become clear.

Trust me!

Not that I am such a pillar of virtue, perhaps, but, as Salazar discovered, I am less untrustworthy than anyone else.

When the chips are down, you must turn to your poets.

In Portugal, the chips have been down for three hundred years!

Besides, if I had invented the exchange, I should have devised something less uncomplimentary to myself.

I have confessed to my feelings for Sidonia. And to my curiosity about her reaction to my plight.

It was not exactly comforting to learn that she'd forgotten my name, my profession, my very existence. "I know no Carlos. I know no poets."

Can you believe that?

Some muse!

◆

Without any recollection whatsoever of that fateful meeting of ours, Sidonia quite naturally assumed that I was simply a figment of the all-too-real Rinaldo, a projected alter ego. . . . That imaginary friend whom we invent when we want to present some humiliating problem. "I have a friend who is pregnant." Or "I have a friend who has knocked up some young lady." Or "I have a friend who has contracted a social disease."

That friend.

She thought that was me. The friend who wrote these mad ravings.

She assumed it would be pornographic. Which would have been interesting because then she could have called the police and had Gomes arrested. She also thought of the fun she could have in showing this long mash note to some of her friends.

At any rate, she assumed it would at least be about her. But she hardly appears in that first section—which was what I'd given Gomes to smuggle out.

She discounted the letter I'd enclosed, believing that to be a part of the fiction.

As any reader might, after all.

The reader is not the writer's friend.

Bored by an implausible story that did not directly concern her and wasn't dirty, she put it somewhere, up in some closet, thinking vaguely that she might be able to use it as evidence in some way if that ridiculous man bothered her again, hanging around in the piazza or calling her up late at night to whisper his fantasies into her ear.

Or to ask her for her soiled underwear.

Her friend Marisa had had that happen to her. Or at least she claimed that it had happened.

Sidonia suspected that Marisa had just read it in a book.

I ought to be fair to Rinaldo, though.

One would infer from Sidonia's reaction that Rinaldo Gomes was insupportably unattractive, that he had some sort of skin problem or nervous tic that would send women fleeing from him.

Not a bit of it. He was a perfectly decent-looking fellow, well turned out, properly tailored and barbered and shod. A little natty, perhaps, but women mostly don't object to excesses in that direction.

It was, in fact, Sidonia's recent experience that had put her in such an unreceptive mood, particularly with a man like Gomes who was, to be candid, somewhat older than she.

As old, say, as Sidonia's father, for instance.

Or as old as any of his friends, colleagues, and business associates.

One of whom, not very long before, had taken Sidonia on a naughty excursion to Taormina, to that famous hotel that used to be a monastery. Where all the old men go with all their young mistresses.

Each of them had gone not so much for the sake of the other as for the sake of who the other was, what the other represented.

For Sidonia, it was a way to show her defiance of her father and assert her independence.

For her father's colleague—one hesitates to call him a friend—it was a way of fucking de Castro. One de Castro could stand in for the other.

The trouble was that he was, as Sidonia reported to her friend Marisa, old and goaty.

Wrinkled all over like a prune. And with a dimply ass that hung down like so much crepe.

Yuck!

When I learned this, I was astonished.

How close I'd been, imagining her on the Costa Smeralda. I'd had the sea right, but I'd got the wrong island.

A mere detail.

Gomes took it personally, of course.

He had failed. Worse than that, he'd succeeded in delivering the manuscript but he'd been made to feel ridiculous.

It was my fault!

He would have enjoyed killing me, or Sidonia, or both of us together.

Unfortunately, however, he had no power to hurt us. We were the ones, he realized, who had power over him. We could destroy him, perhaps get him imprisoned. Surely, we would be putting ourselves at risk as well, but as he saw it, our lives were more or less worthless anyway—a low-level political prisoner and the spoiled daughter of a cork magnate? What were we compared to a man like Rinaldo Gomes?

It was so terribly unfair!

He alternated between states of terror and fury, and mixed with both of these feelings there was the constant chagrin of helplessness. Impotence, one might say, and in connection with a woman like Sidonia, any kind of impotence was a deep affront to the self-esteem of a fellow like Gomes. Those hips and buttocks she twitched so tauntingly were a mockery rather than the invitation Nature had intended.

Those billowy breasts were a nasty graffito on the lavatory wall of his soul!

Excessive? Well, very probably. We poets have our little flights of fancy. And yet, it must be allowed that most of my intimate conversations with Senhor Gomes took place in the lavatory outside the Cabinet Room, where, at adjacent urinals, we discussed the issues of the moment.

"You gave her the manuscript?"

"Yes."

"Good."

"She had no idea who you were. She didn't remember you. You're mad, you know. You've put both our lives into the hands of a stranger. A silly, spoiled, self-indulgent little bitch!"

"Ah, you didn't hit it off? I'm so sorry! Perhaps you aren't her type."

"I can still turn you in. I can turn you both in! I can tell them I wanted to see who your confederates were. And they'll believe me. I'm a Minister of State."

"You were. You aren't anymore. And to whom would you turn us in? Is it still Major Pais who is in charge of the PIDE?"

"You know him?"

"What you mean to ask is whether he knows me. Or whether I am such an abject underling as you have supposed. It is not a question I'm likely to answer, is it?"

He didn't say anything. He merely zipped up.

"Still Pais, then, eh?"

"What difference does it make? They're all the same! When Pais goes, the next one will be no better. Or do you have something on Pais, too?"

I didn't answer. I zipped up, too.

"Perhaps, one day, I shall simply kill you. I have been considering that. It is always a possibility. You push a man too far and he will turn on you, you know. Or a man of honor will. But then, you would not know such people. Scribblers don't associate much with people of dignity and substance, I shouldn't think."

"You are taken in by your own playacting, Senhor. You must try to remember who you are and what your life is about these days. You fool your wife, perhaps. And yourself, evidently. But not me. I'm here, remember. In the same room where the charades are played out, where the farce is enacted week after week, by you people of dignity and substance."

The circulatory system does very interesting things in these moments of crisis. With Gomes, it was amazing to watch his face turn not quite a beet red, but something on the order of salmon pink. And the prominent vein that zigzagged down his forehead bulged out in a menacing and dramatic fashion, suggesting the possibility of some vascular disaster that would leave him lying dead on the tile floor in another couple of seconds.

"Calm yourself," I urged. "Let us return to the council chamber and comport ourselves like . . . the gentlemen we'd like to be."

The little vein throbbed visibly.

Go, little vein!

Imagine it! Not only would Salazar be laid low with his stroke, but his ministers, Gomes first and the others soon thereafter as the fad caught on, all stricken, lying supine and speechless, each of them attended by his *chef de bureau*, and each carted over here, once a week, by ambulance and stretcher, for the weekly meeting of the government.

Thomas Jefferson, the American philosopher, would have approved. After all, the best government is the least government, or so I believe he asserted.

But it is a Portuguese, more than an American, practice. I think of the famous episode in which Pedro the Cruel, one of our illustrious kings, had that special triple throne built for himself, his wife, and the corpse of the mistress his wife had had killed. All summer long, he held court that way, with the corpse in the seat of honor, to his right.

She began to stink, of course.

Pedro affected not to notice.

Depending on how well or badly the members of the cabinet behave, it is quite possible that these meetings could continue, even after Salazar's death. Mercifully, there is refrigeration now.

My own position, of course, would be more precarious. But I pride myself on that. I am a poet, after all.

Which is, by its nature, as precarious as anything I can imagine.

7

I WAS SURPRISED by the decisiveness Salazar displayed. He had had plenty of opportunity to think about his options and make conditional plans beforehand, but with most men there is still some last-minute checking, some reconsideration of what might have been overlooked or underestimated.

Not with Salazar. No sooner had I supplied him with the information he'd asked for than he was ready to go ahead. At the very next cabinet meeting, Dona Maria made one of her appearances, demanded our attention, and announced that Dr. Salazar had decided Major Pais must be removed.

There was consternation.

It wasn't that anyone even thought of arguing with Salazar. That had never happened and, even now (or especially now), was not likely to begin. In their game of Let's Pretend, there hardly seemed to be much point to any real opposition.

Still, they knew they were powerless and would have to lie. Which none of them liked doing.

Especially now that they had become good at it, lying to their wives and children, their mistresses and their friends, and most of all to themselves, about the way they filled up their days in the activities of a mock government.

But they were all still sane enough to understand that Major

Pais was beyond their collective reach. The trouble was, actually, that all of them still found themselves within the ambit of
his authority. And that of the PIDE.

And none of them doubted but that the PIDE received
reports of the deliberations of their meetings. One cannot say,
in the formal way, the Acts—for they had no acts. It was all
talk and nonsense.

Still, some clerk could be keeping track. And any mention
of the name of Silva Pais would be referred upwards, probably
to Pais himself.

Whose revenge might be as intolerable as it was reflexive.

Each of them felt like a flying bug that some meaty hand
could obliterate at any moment—without even involving the
thought process of the huge creature around whose head he was
buzzing.

And there was no way to argue. Or even to ask questions. Of
Dona Maria?

"Are you sure? Dr. Salazar said that?" one finally got up the
nerve to inquire, and Dona Maria nodded.

"He gave no reason?" another asked.

She shook her head. " 'Major Pais must go.' That was all he
said. I have no idea why. I suppose it is for the national good.
Or maybe yours. But it is an effort for him to make himself
understood and he does not explain himself to me these days."

The last phrases were an extravagant Iberian politeness. Had
Salazar ever explained himself to any of them? Or their prede-
cessors? These days or ever?

"What shall we do?" one of the ministers asked.

It was my impression that he was putting the question to his
colleagues, but Dona Maria took it upon herself to prompt
them. It seemed simple enough to her, I imagine.

"Vote," she said.

If that was how she saw it, then that was how she would be
likely to report it to him when they were alone.

Or perhaps that was part of Salazar's instructions to her.

He was lying there, could hear every word they said, and
could be asked to indicate, in the usual way, what he wanted.
Did he want them to vote?

Blink once for yes, twice for no.

But no one had the nerve to confront him, even on the procedural question, let alone the more general issue of what the point could be of so empty an exercise.

After all, they knew that he knew this was all . . . imaginary. That it had nothing to do with the actual government that was meeting and legislating and enforcing and deciding things somewhere else in Lisbon at this very moment.

They voted. To remove Silva Pais.

They would probably have voted to repeal the law of gravity, if that was what Dona Maria had instructed them all to do.

All in favor?

"*Sim,*" they called out.

"Opposed?"

Silence.

I managed not to laugh.

Gomes was probably not the one. Or not one of the several who went carrying tales to the PIDE that afternoon. If it can be said that they were carrying tales to a group and a person who already knew.

Copies of the report were on the desks of Pais and of his boss, the Minister of the Interior, of course, and also on the desk of Caetano himself.

For this was a new thing, a development none of them had considered. It was one thing to provide, out of tact and delicacy of feeling, out of a kind of courtesy, the illusion of a cabinet that still met and considered the problems of the national life and destiny. But to have this feeble old man try to wrest power back into his own hands—or, even worse, his eyelids—that was insupportable.

That was ingratitude, too, they told themselves, as if altruism and respect had been their main motives throughout this business.

Caetano was not going to stand for it! His response was as quick as any of Salazar's ministers could have imagined. Quicker and more decisive.

In a public ceremony, with television cameras and the foreign journalists assembled to witness it, the Minister of the

Interior presented a decoration to Major Silva Pais at PIDE headquarters. The minister then turned the lectern over to Pais, who addressed the press corps and told them that in all of metropolitan Portugal there were no more than 124 "political" prisoners; no one serving a second special "administrative" sentence; and only 31 prisoners presently under interrogation.

Pais then turned the lectern back to the minister, who proclaimed that henceforth there would be no police action against those who merely criticized the government. There was then a reception with champagne and canapés, which sounds like a perfectly civilized way to celebrate the restoration of even a limited degree of civil liberty.

No one believed any of this, of course. But we in the São Bento Palace, in Salazar's suite, understood what had happened. This was Caetano's answer to Salazar's presumption! His chastisement and rebuke.

Or that's what I believed. And I don't think any of the others were much smarter than I was.

I was the one who had to deliver the bad news, though. It was my job to keep Salazar informed—either of the fictional world his cabinet governed or of the actual world of existence of which he'd guessed by means of my injudicious hints and rash jokes.

I told Dona Maria I had to see him, that there was bad news I had to deliver. She did not seem surprised but led me to his chamber and stood back against the wall to wait for me to speak my piece.

I told Salazar how Pais had been decorated. I described the ceremony and the speeches and the unusual invitation of the press to tour the PIDE headquarters.

He looked unperturbed. In fact, it looked as though he were smiling.

No question about it. He was smiling. And the smile grew broader and then erupted into a throaty gargle that Dona Maria assured me, beaming herself, was laughter.

"But why?"

"He fooled them."

"But they didn't get rid of Pais!"

"He didn't want them to. He wanted them to do what they did. And they did it. Exactly as he intended. It was as if he had changed the rules, you see. Now it was twice for yes, once for no. They all fell for it."

I didn't know what to say. I couldn't believe it, but neither could I doubt the fact of Salazar's gurgle of amusement, like the rumbling of plumbing in an old building.

My first thought was—I confess it—of my own hide. Now that the old fox had pulled the wool over the eyes of Caetano's people, there would be penalties extracted, and it appeared to me that I was prime among the candidates for such discipline.

But I was wrong about that, too.

Major Pais came to the palace the next day. To pay his respects. And to thank Salazar.

I was not present at that interview, but I was favored with a brief interview, myself. The chief of the PIDE called for me and had me brought to one of the small reception rooms. One of his aides offered me coffee.

"Thank you, no."

Pais smiled. "You needn't worry. It's not drugged or poisoned."

"No, of course not, Senhor," I protested. "It's just that I am, I confess, a little nervous. . . ."

"Of course. But there is no need for you to be apprehensive. You are a free man."

"I don't understand."

"I had thought," he said, "that a smart fellow like yourself would have figured it out by now. The game is not so very complicated that our old patron has devised. He knew that a man in my position might be uncomfortable during this transitional period. He knew—I like to think—that while I may be obliged on occasion to perform disagreeable tasks for my country, I am, at heart, a man of honor. And he saw his way to doing me a service—for which I am obliged to him."

"You mean, sir, that it was his intention all along to see you confirmed in office?"

"But of course. He knew that our new leaders could only establish their independence of mind by doing something different from what he would have done. His demand that I be dismissed was just the right nudge to get them to confirm me in office in this public way. I could have managed without it, I think, but assuredly it has made my life easier. I am grateful to him, and also to you for the role he tells me you have played."

"And I'm free to go?"

"Quite free. To come and go as you please."

"To travel? Even to leave Portugal for a time?"

"Whatever strikes your poet's soul! You must follow these promptings. It is your vocation."

I had the feeling that he was making fun of me, but I was hardly going to inquire about the depth of his sincerity. It was a subject I could explore at leisure, in that freedom and safety he'd allowed me to imagine.

Major Pais stood, indicating that the little interview was now terminated. I stood too, of course.

"May I ask a question?" I ventured.

"Yes?" He seemed more surprised than annoyed.

"Will those meetings of his former ministers continue?"

"No need," Pais said.

He seemed . . . sad, I think. That struck me as a bit odd, but now that I have had time to consider it, it seems right, too. It was an operation in which he had taken some artistic satisfaction. And, unlike most of the PIDE's assignments, this one had been humanitarian in its purposes. To avoid distressing a respected old man. To save his feelings. To do an act of kindness that would spare him humiliation.

"May I call on Dr. Salazar, to bid him farewell?" I asked.

"That would be decent of you," the major said. "By all means, call on him. At any time."

III

Salazar Does Not Blink

•

1

AND SUDDENLY, JUST LIKE THAT, I WAS FREE.

On somebody's whim.

Which was, I later realized, the problem. If I had been freed on a whim, I could be returned to confinement on a similar caprice. I'd been picked up and stuck into prison in the first place on what still seems to me a flight of fancy. And if it hadn't been for a lucky stroke—Salazar's stroke—I'd probably have been left there to rot.

Throw away the key, as the saying goes.

But they never throw the key away. Even after you're out, they can still come and get you, open the cell door, stick you back in, and lock you up again.

Your freedom is no longer your natural condition, or a human right, but a lucky accident—like good health or prosperity or pleasant weather—and, like all accidents, subject to change.

Mutability. The humors and whimsies not only of Major Pais but of all authorities, mortal and immortal.

I walked out of the São Bento Palace and, by the exercise of considerable self-discipline, managed not to turn around, not to look back. No Orpheus, I. Or Lot's wife either.

But you don't have to look back. The image of the cell marches right along with you, more faithful than a shadow because it clings to you in the darkness, as well as in the light of day. More in the darkness, in fact, because you have to get up during the night to make sure you're out, that you've really been released and haven't just dreamt it.

It would be both reassuring and sobering if we could learn from the sufferings of others—from those millions of souls who have been dragged away in our time either in the dark hours of the night or else in broad daylight with neighbors looking on impassively or even disapprovingly. There is no such thing as the dignity of the human condition. There is no such thing as an inalienable human right. There is only good fortune—the lucky chance that you are not at this moment being persecuted. That you and your people are not this week being done to death.

If people were as smart as we pretend to be, as generous or as caring, we'd all have gone mad long ago.

But no one believes what he reads in the papers or hears on the radio or sees on television. One could hardly bear all that horror if it were true, were in some way relevant, or could affect one, afflicting one the way it has its victims, with random savagery.

One's own life is different. Must be different.

Well, that's what I thought. And then, after my imprisonment—brief, actually, and comparatively very comfortable—I was no longer immune, no longer protected or in any way different from any other victim.

I didn't have to look around because I knew the PIDE was watching me, following me, and that they could at any moment, and for no reason at all, pounce, seize me, stick me back into the Aljube. Or shoot me like a dog and throw my body into the Tagus.

The worst of it was that this new way of thinking about life was not delusional. I wasn't paranoid or . . . What is the word they use? "Inappropriate"? The illness is the other way, in not realizing how precarious life is, in failing to understand how lucky one is to be able to walk the streets without looking around or sleep in one's bed without listening for the breaking of glass, the smashing of doors, or the sounds of boot-shod footsteps coming up the stairs.

◆

And there was one other problem.

There was another copy of the manuscript I'd made, in case Gomes threw it away, or burned it, or fled with it to Goa. I'd left that copy of the manuscript behind, hidden in the gardener's tool shed.

I hadn't forgotten it. One doesn't just forget a project that has been sanity's ballast. (It is not up to me to pass qualitative judgment on its literary merits—which were unimportant compared with the psychological and philosophical value of the account I'd been compiling of my experiences.) I just hadn't had the nerve to go and get it, not while they were watching me, anyway. And I was reluctant to hang around. I didn't want to risk their possible change of heart.

Not that my behavior ever had anything much to do with their decisions. But one tends to slip into a naive belief in cause and effect. If they punish, then one must in some way have deserved it, having sinned somehow even if in some other context. Maybe even in some other life.

So I didn't want to be a pest. I just wanted to get the hell out of there.

At the worst, I could sit down and recreate the manuscript, remembering what I could, creating anew what I had to.

Shrewd or just craven, I decided simply to walk away, without looking back, and I even managed not to run until I had disappeared around the first corner.

Besides, as I realized only a little later, Sidonia had a copy— at least of the first part of it.

If Gomes hadn't lied, that is, when he claimed to have given it to her.

I could get it from her.

Even if, as he'd said, she didn't remember me?

Even then, and assuming that she had no idea who I was, and didn't even believe that I existed, I could still present myself, make a brief but persuasive representation of the facts, and ask for her indulgence and generosity.

Over and over, I thought of that confrontation, telling myself it wasn't so dreadful, that any reasonable and decent person would, without hesitation, restore a writer's work to him. Why on earth not?

After all, I had for a brief time thought of Sidonia as my muse.

But that was the trouble. One prays to the muse not because she is so reliably generous and forthcoming but because she is not. One prays, I'm afraid, because she is grudging, inconstant, indifferent, fickle, vain, stupid, desirable but promiscuous, flighty, bitchy . . .

All of these turned out to be precisely the qualities of Sidonia de Castro!

But before I commenced my quest for the missing pages, I had other even more pressing business to transact. I had to find a place to live, for instance. My old apartment had been leased to a new, more desirable, more reliable tenant—I could hardly blame my landlady, who had had no reason to assume I would ever return. I had reason to be grateful in fact for her consideration inasmuch as she had not carted my books and papers off to the dump but had carefully packed them away and stored them in what had once been the carriage house and was now a garage for her little Fiat.

Thank God the car didn't take up much room and that there was a considerable area that remained as a depot for junk. And I thanked my former landlady, too.

"No, no, don't thank me," she said. "I did it only because I thought there might be something of value there."

"Most considerate," I said.

"No, I'd call it desperate," she answered. "But you can have it all as soon as you pay me the back rent you owe."

We haggled over that. She wanted rent for all the time I'd been in prison. I was willing to make up for what she'd actually lost between my being taken away and her getting the new tenant.

She didn't sound happy about it, but she was still doing better than she had expected. I promised her I'd bring the money as soon as I could. She said I had a week before she started adding storage charges to what I already owed.

"It's junk anyway," she said. "If I'd been sane, I should have burned it all."

"You're most kind," I said, "most gracious."

"And I will burn it, too, if you don't show up with the money."

"I'm obliged to you," I told her. "Deeply obliged."

She snorted and slammed the door not quite in my face.

Later that afternoon, I managed to find an old friend and occasional collaborator—a photographer who sometimes took pictures of what I wrote about—whose arm I could twist until he agreed to let me bunk down on the sofa in his living room for a few days. My friend, Xavier, was hardly enthusiastic about this arrangement. I had been arrested, after all, and there was a taint to me now, as if I had had some social disease that was not altogether cured and might flare up in new pustules, and, more to the point, spread its contagion to innocent people like himself. I told him that I'd had a cordial conversation with Major Pais himself, and was now perfectly free to come and go as I pleased. The misunderstanding—which was all it had been—had been sorted out to everyone's satisfaction, I assured him.

He didn't seem quite convinced.

"Just until I find my own place," I pleaded. "A few days, I promise."

"All right," he agreed, but it was clearly against his better judgment.

If I'd been in his situation, I should have had my hesitations, too.

There were yet other details to attend to. I had to get hold of some money, not only to pay off my former landlady but also to live on. This wasn't quite so difficult as I thought it might be. My taint was a weapon I could use to good effect. I could get people to give me money in exchange for nothing more than my assurance that I'd steer clear of them. I promised to repay, of course, but they didn't take these promises seriously. All they really wanted from me was that I should give them as wide a berth as possible. They wanted never to see me again.

And, of course, once I understood that, I realized I could hit up a fair number of people for small- and medium-sized sums, simply by showing up where they least wanted to be seen with me, at their places of business or at their homes.

Which was how I came to realize that my relationship with Rinaldo Gomes had perhaps not yet absolutely exhausted itself. If my old friends, who had no way of guessing the nature of my recent activities, wanted to avoid the contagion I brought with me, Senhor Gomes, who knew exactly what I had been doing, had all the more reason for keeping far away from me. After all, I knew what he'd been up to all this time.

His pointless days, his empty attaché case, his betrayal of his old master and his servility to his new ones, his utterly abject and contemptible spinelessness . . . I had seen into the cesspool of his soul!

How fitting that our only conversations had been at adjacent urinals in a men's room.

I think it was the morning of my second day of liberty that I took a bus to within a couple of blocks of his house and then walked up a hill and found the building. He had a fashionable address, an imposing facade, and through the grillwork of the gate I could see a well-kept garden of some charm. I pulled the crank that sounded a bell within. An old woman in servant's black answered the door, and I gave my name and asked her to let Senhor Gomes know I wanted to see him.

She glared at me. Obviously, this was irregular. Few people arrived on foot this way and presumed to ask for an interview with the master.

"It's all right," I assured her. "He'll want to see me."

"Wait!" she told me and disappeared, not even inviting me into the garden but leaving me outside the gate, still peering through the wrought iron grill.

He appeared, just as I thought he would. "You!" he exclaimed, not at all pleased.

"We need to talk," I told him.

"You may need to talk. I don't. I don't want to see you ever again."

"Would you prefer me to write an article about the cruel hoax you all played on a sick old man?"

"Write whatever you please!"

"Very well," I said, turning away.

I took three steps. A fourth.

"Wait," he called out. "Come back!"

I should have made him say "Please," but I had more important games to play.

I could describe the scene in a way that would be flattering to myself. One is always tempted in that direction.

But what happened was even more interesting, full of the wonderful unpredictability I used to love in books and that drew me to literature in the first place. All those amazing reversals, the disasters narrowly averted, the wicked plots foiled by physical courage or mental shrewdness, or best of all just by the shining glow of a hero's virtuous character.

I don't claim any such heroic qualities for myself. What I had was a willingness to trust to the rough justice of the situation, the likely issue of his instincts and my own on the bumpy playing field on which we found ourselves. In a crude way, yes, I was trusting that my character would somehow triumph over his.

To put it another way, I had no plan.

But then, I didn't need one. Gomes attacked first. He was furious.

"You will not write any articles. You will not breathe a word about what has happened—not even to your mother. You writer fellows think you are so clever, but the opposite is true— you are fools, dreamers and fools. You think you can blackmail me, but it won't work. All you have to do is drop the slightest hint about what has happened, and you will be back in the Aljube so fast it will make your head spin."

"You think so?" I asked, enjoying myself. I wanted to let him run on, digging himself deeper into the pit with each orotund period.

"I know so!" he said. We were like schoolboys taunting one another in a playground. "You can't expose me without ruining yourself, which you won't do . . . because you don't have the balls for it."

"You peeked, at the urinals?" I teased. "I hate people who do that!"

He glared at me, dismayed that I had required him to operate at such a vulgar level. He was not so sure of himself there, perhaps. "I'm surprised at you," I continued. "I'd have thought you were one of the shy ones who keeps his eyes front and worries about being misunderstood if he were to look around."

"Get out," he said, very quietly. "Go and write your article. No one will believe you anyway. And you will only be writing your own lettre de cachet."

"Very well," I said, cheerfully enough. "But I will play fair with you. I ought to mention that I spoke earlier this week with Major Pais—whom I invite you to call. Ask him whether we did not have a friendly talk. Ask him if there were any restrictions that were put on my freedom, any conditions, any suggestion of any kind that I should keep quiet about certain recent amusing events. He will tell you what I am telling you. And you will believe him. But it will be too late. And when you then call to ask my pardon and my help, I may not be in so generous and forthcoming a mood as you find me at this moment."

It was lovely. There was a sudden deflation. Or, no, that suggests a balloon with the air escaping. This was even more absolute—as with an animal that has been killed, that has been turned from creature to meat, but still stands there for a brief moment, waiting with the admirable patience of any inanimate thing for the force of gravity to decide which way it will fall.

And then, it collapses.

2

PERHAPS I HAVE BEEN TOO SEVERE?

As I consider it now, friend Rinaldo had good reason to worry when I appeared at his gate that morning. Knowing how precarious he must have felt his situation, I suppose that there was a certain degree of desperate courage in his decision to attack me that way. Or his instinct.

His habit, perhaps? Bluster must have been one of his more reliable instrumentalities of interaction. Treat the world as an underling and it will behave like one—most of the time.

But occasionally it will snarl, snap, and bite you in the ass.

Even that improbable outcome, however, now seems to me capable of another and more generous interpretation. After all, Rinaldo Gomes was never a deep thinker. His mind, as far as I have deigned to explore it, was a barren patch of broad-leafed platitudes and scrub pieties. He was, I swear, a patriotic Portuguese—and that, as much as anything else, was his undoing.

What he was unable to imagine was the national shamelessness. Nobody cared about my manuscript because nobody saw it as a possible affront to the national honor. Salazar had been grossly deceived? Fine! It served him right!

His cabinet—which had been, after all, our government—

was revealed to be a herd of craven toadies? We all knew it all along. Who ever thought otherwise?

The makers of the national policy, both before and after the stroke, were revealed to be a group of fantasy mongers? That has been true ever since Dom Sebastião was lost (or perhaps only mislaid?) somewhere among the carnage of that battlefield in Morocco.

What Senhor Gomes couldn't quite bring himself to admit, because it would have diminished the outrageousness of what he'd done and the gravity of his deeds and misdeeds, was that nobody gave a damn. Nobody took the government seriously or suspected that its discussions and decisions were worth much attention.

Which is, of course, the mistake that all governmental officials make.

The depradations of the tax collector and of the army and the police—those are serious. But those are not policy. Those are more like the ravages of locusts or the annoying raids of mosquitoes. There's hardly a policy question to debate or examine. And governments are just one more form of pestilence.

But those in the government—with their limousines and their big desks and impressive offices—never see it that way.

They fool themselves first.

Salazarismo.

I'm not criticizing old Rinaldo, here. Not on these grounds. I can't afford to. I have to confess that I too supposed we had a secret we shared, the telling of which might be our undoing. I have to confess that I supposed, along with him, that the PIDE would not want it noised about in the land that this satyr play had been going on, inside the palace and, by extension, outside it, too, for months.

For all our lifetimes.

"What is it that you want of me?" Gomes asked at last.

"Take me to Sidonia," I told him.

"You can't be serious."

"I am. Absolutely."

"But she is your friend. You were the one who sent her that manuscript."

"And did she know who I was?"

"She said she didn't," Gomes admitted. "But I hardly believed that. Not at all. Not for a moment. Why would you send your manuscript to a stranger? Why would you trust her with it? Why would you implicate her?"

"Why would I implicate a friend?" I asked him.

He chewed that over for a second or two. Then he started to laugh. "She doesn't know you? That's wonderful!"

"I'm glad you're amused," I told him.

"And she thought I was an old reprobate," he said, "some common masher who was pestering her. . . ." He laughed again, a kind of high whinny, or call it a schoolboy giggle. It was, at any rate, the first evidence I'd had of some recognizable humanity.

"Ridiculous!" he said, when he'd regained control of himself. "Stupid. Dumb!"

"You or me?" I asked.

"Both. All. Everything. Everyone. You didn't know her? Truly?"

"I'd met her, but that's all. Whether she remembered me or not, I certainly remembered her. And now I need to see her. You gave her the manuscript, didn't you? She actually has it?"

"I gave it to her," he said. "Whether she kept it or threw it away, I couldn't guess," he told me.

"We'll find out, won't we?"

"I expect so," he said drily.

On our way over to the café near where Sidonia lived, Senhor Gomes asked me why I'd picked her. Had it been more or less at random?

"Not at all," I told him, honestly. "There is an apparent randomness, I suppose, but that's true of all the important events in our lives, is it not? As I say, I'd met her at a party. I knew who she was. We talked for a few moments."

"And that was all? You loved her at first sight? Or hated her?"

"Yes. Exactly," I said.

"But which?"

"Both," I said. "Or to be clearer, I should say I loved her but didn't like her much. Or even at all. I disapproved of her, I suppose. All that money and nothing to do with it except amuse herself. Indulge herself. I hated that. Or envied it."

"*Fado!*" he said, meaning Fate and the respect we Portuguese allow it, even in our popular culture.

"Exactly," I said.

We drove for a little while and then he said to me, "You know, this is not going to be so easy."

"Why not?"

"She doesn't know you. And she thinks I'm some sort of a pervert. Which of us is to introduce the other? Have you thought about that?"

"No."

"I'll do whatever you want. But you have to decide what that is."

"I'll think of something."

"I hope so," he said.

So I was thinking. He was thinking, too, which was surprising. I don't mean that it was surprising for him to be able to think. It's only that this was my difficulty, my problem, and he had come along only to satisfy me—not even because of my threats but because we now had a kind of relationship. We knew disgraceful things about one another, and while that may not have been the whole basis of the association, it wasn't irrelevant either.

We were like two young men out on the town together who are trying to find some pretext to address some attractive young woman they have been staring at from a distance. Either of them, on his own, might just give up and slink away. Together, though, they are bound to go forward, because neither can let the other suspect him of faintheartedness. Or lack of self-assurance. It becomes a contest of nerve, and the girl is almost secondary.

The little square with a fountain at its center and a small café on one side with brightly painted chairs beneath a striped awning, with housewives on their way home carrying their groceries in those network sacks . . . they all seemed like a stage set constructed for our benefit, intended only to lend some air of plausibility to the odd transaction with which we were occupied.

I remember that feeling of curiosity a member of an audience might have experienced, wondering what the next lines of witty dialogue would be and the next twist of an already excessively contrived plot.

We sat there together for rather a long time, drinking coffee and exchanging small talk. And some talk that was not so small. Now that Gomes understood I was not determined on his ruin, he was prepared to grant me at least a little human recognition. "It must have been difficult for you, locked up that way and making those broadcasts. . . ."

"Not so bad," I told him. "It was better than being a prisoner in the Aljube. It wasn't physically uncomfortable. It was . . . ridiculous. But then, what you had to do was also ridiculous. Neither of us was comfortable."

"That's true," he said, "but one must recognize one's limitations. When there is no other way, it is sometimes necessary to yield in order to survive. Even to ridiculousness."

"Of course," I agreed.

"We pretend it isn't so. That we'd fight to the death over a matter of honor. But luckily we are not small boys anymore. We don't have to be stupid."

"Did you and the other ministers see much of each other when you were not at the palace?" I asked.

"No, no. We avoided each other."

"Perhaps it would have been better if you had not. If you had found ways to encourage your friends and colleagues, if you had been . . . fellow sufferers, supporting one another."

"If it had gone on longer," he said, "that might have happened. Who knows?"

"But nearly a year!"

He nodded. He signaled the waiter for more coffee. And then, with his hand still extended to catch the waiter's attention, he moved the finger from upright to pointing. "There she is. Your Sidonia!"

Abruptly, Gomes got up, approached her, and called out, "Senhorita, a thousand pardons. But there he is, that man I have been talking about. That crazy person! You see? He exists. I promise, I will trouble you no further. It is all his doing. He alone is responsible."

And then, he turned and took off. He fled. He'd been sitting and talking, but all the time he'd been planning what he'd say and then what route he'd use to disappear.

And of course I could not pursue him, for if I did so it would mean that I too would be running away from the woman to whom he had just introduced me—although with rather less ceremony than I might have liked.

"Senhorita," I said. "If you will allow me just a moment of your time . . ."

She was puzzled but she did not feel herself to be endangered in so public a place. And she was amused. "Do I know you?" she asked.

"We met at a party a couple of years ago," I said. "I don't expect you'd remember."

She shook her head.

I was dismayed. I hadn't expected her to remember me, but unless I made some sort of impression and quickly retrieved my ruinous losses, she'd just walk away and my manuscript would be gone forever. What made it all the more difficult was that she was at least as gorgeous as I had remembered. She was a bit chunkier, a little earthier than what I had been able to summon up, combining popular images of beauty with my memory of her actual appearance. But the air was right, the self-assurance, the burnished tan, the impressively well-groomed look of the rich and pampered. She was a bit broad in the hips and big in the bosom and yet she didn't look bovine. She wore her body like a piece of costume jewelry—which is a trick the rich have. I remembered the same terrible feeling of being awestruck and tongue-tied. And here I was, years later, no better prepared than the last time.

"You said I looked like a druggist," I reminded her, thinking of that other time.

She furrowed her brow.

"I am the poet . . ." I began, but at that declaration she smiled. Her face changed. She laughed, almost as if she were continuing with the same peal of laughter that had been so hurtful at that party, long ago.

"I remember now," she said. "Yes, yes. I remember you."

"I am grateful," I said.

"And from that meeting you sent me your book of poems?"

I acknowledged that this is exactly what had happened. And then I asked her the question I most feared to ask, "Did Senhor Gomes give you the manuscript?"

"Oh, yes."

"And you still have it? You haven't thrown it away?"

She shook her head.

"It's very funny," she said.

"Funny?" I asked. "That I should send it to you?"

"That, too, but I meant the book," she said. "I read it. I laughed a lot."

"I'm glad to hear it," I said, thinking her heartless. My sufferings were funny! It is not what one hopes to hear from one's muse. "My copy has been lost," I told her. "And I hoped you might be willing to give me yours, or at least to lend it to me so that I might make a copy. . . ."

She looked at me, trying to decide.

"I was wrong," she said. "You don't look like a druggist. You're fatter than you should be, but you have sad eyes. You could be a poet."

"Thank you," I said.

She sat down at the seat Gomes had vacated. "Buy me a coffee," she said.

I ordered coffees.

"Now," she said, "tell me why did you send the manuscript to me? Why me, of all people?"

"Because I love you," I said, taking a desperate gamble.

She laughed again. "Wonderful!" she said. "You really are a very funny man!"

3

CLEARLY, SHE THOUGHT I WAS INSINCERE. What was less clear was whether this assumption on her part was prompted by fear or hope. Was I yet another smooth-talking seducer, not even trying very hard to deceive her, but content to say the conventional things the usual way for the usual reward? Or was I so pathetic and gauche as to be saying what I thought to be true—in which case I would not do, not even for an evening's entertainment.

Bored, spoiled, looking for a new treat as she scanned the menu that life's headwaiter had handed her, she considered the possibilities my bizzare appearance might offer. I was not particularly promising, perhaps, but then what the chef does in the kitchen is crucial. Otherwise, who would want to eat sweetbreads, brains, kidneys, and other offal? The right sauce, the proper presentation, and one may turn near garbage into a delicacy!

So, perhaps because of my unprepossessing air, she decided I was interesting.

Which may have been, I decided, what Gomes had banked on.

I thought, at first, that he'd simply betrayed me, that he'd been waiting to blurt out to her that I was a maniac and then run away, just as he did. But what could he have dreamed up that would have better recommended me? She had been anything but encouraging to him, on his own. He could not suppose that his introduction would carry much weight with her or be of any great value to me. So to establish distance between us, to let her know that he and I were anything but friends and confederates was the greatest favor he could have done me.

Did he know that? Or did it just work out that way?

No way to decide. Nor is there any need to. It is simply a matter of what one's preference is, how one looks at the world and what one chooses to believe about its way of working.

I choose to believe that he was not trying to be helpful, but that, despite himself, he did me the best service he could have done.

Sidonia allowed me to buy her a coffee, listened while I explained to her how we had met, and even—I could hardly believe my luck—invited me to call upon her at home that very evening.

I accepted, of course.

"Now, tell me again, about your love for me."

"You are making light of serious emotion," I warned her.

"One of us is," she said.

"I think it was the combination of your great beauty and your haughtiness. Your cynicism."

"You admired that?"

"It made me rather sad. I thought of you as . . . as in need of a kind of love I could offer you."

"A different path but it leads to the usual conclusion, does it not?"

"Very probably."

"And I thought you poets were supposed to be so clever."

"A different path to the usual conclusion is as clever as most of us want to be," I told her.

"We'll see whether that's clever enough," she said. "Come at ten, if that's convenient." She gave me the address and pointed to the building. She thanked me for the coffee and batted her eyes in a stagy way. "Until tonight, then, lover."

People were looking at us. I couldn't decide whether she was trying to embarrass me or let me preen a little before the onlookers.

But what choice had I? The only thing for it was to preen. Which I did, grinning broadly as I called for the check.

I thought again of Rinaldo, understanding him and how he had been reduced to awkwardness by the dazzling glare of her beauty. Actually, it had been worse for him than it was for me, because he had a certain dignity to maintain, having to comport himself at all times as a minister of state . . . because his attitude and deportment were the entire contents of his portfolio. The first shadow of doubt—his own or anyone else's—and he was removed from office.

A minister and also a husband, and if he had once won Luisa by his assertion of self-confidence, he ran the risk with Sidonia of losing that entitlement, which would either lose him his beloved Luisa or else—and probably worse—diminish her, reduce her further in status to the spouse of an ordinary fellow of no particular quality or refinement.

A married man owes it to his wife to pick his mistresses with discrimination and refinement, maintaining some standards of taste and judgment. By the same token, he owes it to his wife never to be a rejected suitor.

I had no such impediments. As a poet, I could wallow in the muck of experience without fear of embarrassment. Poets are expected to wallow in muck. That's where people suppose the poetry comes from.

I expect it does, sometimes.

But I am getting it wrong again. To adore Sidonia is not to wallow in muck. It is to aspire grandly, and only incidentally to risk an abject falling into the abyss of self-contempt. For without her, what else can life offer? What comparable elevation can there be? Even to be the butt of Sidonia's jokes and the object of her laughter is to be ennobled. Better to be laughed at by that beautiful woman than to be enshrined in the national portrait gallery and have one's bust gracing the bookcases of schoolrooms all over Portugal for decades, for centuries to come.

Better to be invited to Sidonia's apartment at ten o'clock than to be invited to join Camões and Almeida Garrett in the pages of the *Literary History of Portugal!*

God, yes!

Obviously, I hardly knew the young woman. This was an impediment in some ways, but there was also a degree of freedom I enjoyed at this stage, an ability for instance to fantasize as I pleased without the hindrance of dreary facts and sordid probabilities. I could suppose, for instance, that she might in some way feel flattered by the accident of my having addressed my manuscript to her. It was even probable that she should have such a reaction. I mean, part of my decision was based on my reluctance to compromise any of my friends. And part was my assumption that a girl of her wealth and family connections could avoid trouble or, at worst, buy her way out of it more easily than a less fortunate individual might.

But partly I was actually responding in my bumbling and approximate way to her poise and her beauty. I had actually thought of her as a kind of muse.

She might like that. She might find it fun—like those fun furs that northern women wear to sporting events or just to go shopping in. The animal is just as dead, of course, but there is a place in the closet's shrine for the pelt. By that kind of reasoning, and feeling as stricken as I did, I could entertain a pale hope that she might elect to reward me . . . not out of passion, surely, or even any spirit of adventure, but for a lark.

As an amusement.

An entremets, to clear the palate.

The hour was not discouraging, surely. Ten o'clock? At her apartment? I could imagine the champagne chilling in the bucket, caviar in the crystal server on its bed of ice, and grated egg whites and minced onions and dark capers attractively disposed in a segmented dish of great age and delicacy.

Candlelight, of course.

And through an open door, just a glimpse of the bed with its satin coverlet turned down to show a flash of lace pillow slip and embroidered bed linen.

Why not? Such things happen to other men.

Why not to me, too?

Even if she were to laugh during the entire exercise, I should not feel badly used.

Well, almost the entire exercise . . .

I cannot remember how I got through those intervening hours. I know I spent a fair amount of the time imagining what our rendezvous would be like. That we had a rendezvous was the main thing, the nub of fact around which I could embellish as I pleased. I know I spent some considerable time choosing what I would wear, constructing from my rather limited repertoire the most sophisticated ensemble I could devise—a serviceable suit and a good shirt but no tie. I shined my shoes. I took a long, hot bath to prepare my body for whatever good fortune might befall its crevices and protuberances, its public expanses and its more secret places. I remember looking at myself in the flattering blur of a steamy mirror and deciding that I was not exactly fat but only ample. One might even go so far as to say generous. Abundant, even. But not fat.

Anyway, Sidonia was no sylph. Better than that, she had a lovely feminine *gravitas* that was beyond the whimsical dictates of the doyennes of fashion. She and I would be a matched pair!

The time dragged. But it did eventually pass, and I found myself back in that little square, sitting at the same café and waiting for my watch to tell me not only that it was time but that I was a few minutes late. I didn't want to appear too impossibly eager. Give it ten minutes, I told myself. Or at least five.

Yes, five would do.

Ah, but it was difficult. Nevertheless, I forced myself to watch as the second hand lurched forward, digging in its heels at every gear tooth of the wheel to which it was attached. An exquisite kind of suffering, but eventually it yielded to my importunate staring, showed pity to my distress, and allowed me to get up and march toward her building—but slowly, slowly, no running, or she will see through you and throw you out for your naughty thoughts and terrible manners! And how will you like that, you miserable excuse for a poet, you impostor, you joke of a gallant?

I was already flustered by the time I rang the doorbell, so I could not have been much further disturbed when I discovered that we were not, after all, to share the evening by ourselves, tête-à-tête. There were just a few others.

Perhaps thirty? All of them young and rich and smart and bored. Like Sidonia herself.

She wanted to share me with them. To show me off.

More likely, she thought it would be fun if they all laughed at me together.

My smile froze. It really did. I could feel it wither and die, and I consciously held the muscles to preserve the baboon's rictus that was the best I could manage.

She introduced me around to those who were closest to the door, but then gave up. "You'll meet whom you like," she told me. "We're all easy here."

"You are too kind," I said. It was a joke line from school, something one said in answer to an insult. Sidonia did not know the joke. Or knowing it, she didn't care. She nodded in the direction of the bar. "Get yourself something to drink," she suggested.

"Thank you," I said.

Thank God, I had not gone to the florist. And had decided against a tie. And for a thousand other tiny favors so that I did not look as ridiculous as I felt.

French cognac. Scotch whiskey. Jamaican rum. Various kinds of liqueurs and eaux-de-vie. I fixed myself a very large whiskey of a brand I can seldom afford. I turned to toast her and say something witty, but she had already disappeared.

4

THERE COMES A TIME in every man's life when it dawns on him that he is the oldest man at the party.

And with that realization, there is a moment of struggle. On the one hand, it is obvious that these youngsters don't know anything, that they are callow and brash and—let's be candid—stupid. But on the other hand, they own the world, their youth and grace and beauty, however unearned and however temporary, giving them title to all the delights and worldly pleasures to which one is not quite ready, oneself, to bid farewell.

This was, for me, such an occasion. I wandered from group to group and from room to room, not much noticed, I'm sorry to say, but with a certain degree of freedom to observe, to listen in, to eavesdrop. The young men and women, Sidonia's friends, were as hard in their judgments as in their bellies. A woman I used to know of a certain age but of remarkable erotic gifts used to refer to such people as "flat-tummied monsters." And it's true, I realized, while at the same time admitting that they were desirable.

One wanted to ruffle their smooth surfaces, disturb that sleekness and produce in those impossibly smooth brows the wrinkles of perplexity and distress that are our badges of humanity. They were like wet concrete in which one feels impelled to scrawl one's initials.

The young men were all preening, showing off their knowledge of horses and cars and food and wines, strutting like peacocks before the young women who hardly bothered to conceal the fact that they were bored, who didn't even find their boredom remarkable but rather supposed it to be the human condition. Boredom and satiety. Where to go for the weekend? Where to swim? Where to wind surf? Where to scuba dive? Where to hang glide? They were not looking for opportunities for athletic activities but for a more spiritual set of rewards—a little excitement, perhaps a little danger, and at the same time, an opportunity to be chic, to wear the right clothing and drink this season's preferred aperitif.

It could have been staged for a layout in some fashion magazine or an illustration in an advertisement that offers, along with whatever product, youth and gaiety and liveliness. . . . The trouble was that it didn't strike me as all that gay or lively. It was depressing. It was all but intolerable. I wondered whether Sidonia had assembled these people for some didactic purpose, to demonstrate to me that my manuscript was irrelevant. This wasn't likely. There were too many people here. The party had been laid on some time ago and only on impulse had she thought to include me, perhaps because there was some kind of safety in inviting me to her apartment when it was full of her friends. Still, it was tempting to suppose that there was some deeper intention on someone's part, some subtle intelligence using the occasion to make its philosophical suggestion—that for one thing, there were as many different dream Portugals as there were dreamers. That all Portuguese are dreamers, the young and the rich as well as the old and the poor.

Except, evidently, the poets, who feel it necessary to rouse them from their torpor, to shake them awake, to prod and poke them until they are forced to recognize the truth that surrounds them, their landscape and their heritage—and either admit it and accommodate it or else try to do something to change it.

This is exactly the reverse of what we have been led to expect, but such reversals are often the way to the truth, are they not?

I sipped at my whiskey and felt its effect on me. I had not been able to drink for some months and I was more susceptible to it than usual. I listened to the snatches of conversation that swirled around me until I could no longer put up with the drivel I was hearing. I decided that if there was any message from Sidonia in the evening's assembly, it was to let me know that this was her world and these were her friends, that I had misjudged her, that I had imposed upon an entirely inappropriate person with my bizarre story of the stricken Salazar. . . .

Perhaps she was right. And yet, what could I do, stricken as I had been by her beauty and her suave assurance that the world was her plaything? I couldn't just take my manuscript and go. I had to hold out some helping hand to rescue her from the inanity of this life she was flaunting before me.

A daunting prospect. And the odds of my success were not great. I knew that. And therefore, I decided to attempt some interchange with one of Sidonia's companions, hoping in this trial run to glean some helpful information that might improve on those long odds. I might learn at least what didn't work, what moves I ought to avoid.

I think it is accurate to say that these were the thoughts in my mind. I had been drinking, but it was not altogether an impulsive reply I made when one of the young ladies asked me where I had vacationed this past winter.

"I've been in prison, actually," I said, admirably matter-of-fact.

"Really?" she asked, not quite sure whether to believe me. Or, if she did believe it, whether to feel sympathy or distaste.

"In the Aljube, for a while. And then in the São Bento Palace."

"That's hardly a prison," the young man beside her corrected me. He had pomaded hair in the fashion of the silent-film stars of the twenties, Ramon Novarro and Rudolph Valentino. And he displayed a pair of sunglasses that were tucked into the neck of his pastel polo shirt as if they were his recently validated visa.

"It didn't use to be," I agree. "But since Dr. Salazar's stroke, it has become a kind of fortress. His cabinet still meets, you know. Three times a week. And they pretend to govern the country. Or we pretend that they aren't doing that."

"You don't say!" the young woman said, taking a swig of the amber-colored liquid in her tumbler with which she included an ice cube that she dandled for a moment on her tongue and then let drop back into her drink. The young man with the sunglasses observed this transaction intently, perhaps with the knowledge that it would soon enough be his turn for such treatment.

"I was there," I insisted.

She raised an index finger and with it described a small ascending spiral in a gesture of sarcastic applause.

"That doesn't concern you?" I asked them.

"Not particularly," the fellow with the sunglasses answered.

"That we have had an imaginary government for the past year or so? That we have had an imaginary government in one sense or another since 1924?"

He did a stagy yawn.

"Or that men and women are dying in Africa, acting out our nightmares for us?"

"I had nothing to do with that," the young man said. "And Feliciana certainly had nothing to do with it. She is too much occupied with her own nightmares. Isn't that so?"

On cue, she produced the appropriate shy smile, like that of a little child who has been caught out in a mischief.

"And you think they are not related," I asked, "the country's nightmares and your own?"

"No," she said.

"You're bothering her," the young man decided.

"A good thing, perhaps?"

"Not a good thing! Fuck off!"

"Too kind," I said, and I headed back to the bar for a refill.

Sidonia, I now discovered, had been standing behind me, enjoying the interchange.

"I don't understand your friends," I told her.

"Or they you," she said.

"I don't think I like them."

"Or they you."

"And I'm a little puzzled that you like them," I said, pressing it a bit.

She shrugged. "Does one pick one's friends? Or do they only happen?"

"I thought it was relatives that just happened. Of course one picks one's friends."

"I don't know. Did I pick you? Did you pick me, for that matter? Didn't we just happen?"

"Are we friends?" I asked.

She shrugged as if it were not important. "I had hoped for more fireworks," she said. "I thought you would be angrier. That you would get up on your high horse and that one of them would knock you down somehow."

"Is that what you wanted?"

"It would have been a happening. I thought that if there could be a fight, I could help you. Or throw you out. I could tell better whether I liked you or hated you."

"You need a fight to help you make up your mind?" I asked. "All I want is to borrow my manuscript back for a while," I told her. "After that, I won't bother you anymore."

"No, that's not all you want, is it?" She looked at me through narrowed lids, frankly appraising.

I didn't have to think about it very hard. I wanted to take her away from these stupid and trivial people. I wanted to keep her from turning into one of them. I wanted to save her somehow. I confessed, "No, perhaps not."

"You need another drink," she suggested.

"Yes," I agreed. But instead of getting myself the drink, I asked her, "Do you like these people? Are you like these people?"

"Are they so terrible?"

"They are not serious. They don't take serious things seriously."

She just laughed.

I got myself another Scotch. "Anything for you?" I asked her.

"I'm fine," she said, putting her hands into the pockets of her voluminous peasant skirt, leaning against the doorframe, and crossing one leg in front of the other.

"Do I get to talk to you in private?" I asked.

"In time, perhaps. Be a little patient. And serious!"

"All right.'

"Circulate!" she told me.

"All right."

I wandered about from group to group and from room to room. There were dishes full of food on the large refectory table in the dining room. There were hors d'oeuvres in the living room and in the studio. On all the walls, there were objects of art—mostly folk art, tiles, or pieces of woven cloth—or photographs of fence posts against an empty sky. There was a bookcase in the studio with a small collection of volumes of which I could make no sense. *The Second Sex* and *Story of O* were standing cheek to cheek.

The guests were all obviously jeunesse dorée who always seem lucky and blessed, but in a poor country like ours must appear even more unrelated to the real world outside. Being older than they, I resented them and then found myself arguing their case in that mental court of mine that is permanently in session. They were perhaps right to behave this way, I found myself thinking, because they had the same feelings that I had about their good fortune—that it was unearned, that they could lose their precarious advantages at any time. I told myself that these were decent and sympathetic people once and that they had been required by their wealth and their good luck to harden themselves, to learn not to see and hear and smell the suffering around them. For the sake of their very sanity they have had to learn the tricks of tyrants—not because they are, themselves, tyrants but because they were once spontaneous and charitable people with generous impulses and enlightened ideas about how men and women ought to live together.

Like people in pain, they spend a great deal of their energy trying to distract themselves, which is why it is so important to

them if a new rock singer from Liverpool or a new designer
from Paris offers some small possibility of novelty, gives them
some occasion for a momentary enthusiasm.

Their elders, including no doubt some of the men who had
been meeting in Salazar's bedroom, were already hardened to
their choices, the exclusions they had contrived and the dimi-
nutions they had accepted in exchange for the money and
power by which they defined themselves. For their children,
the same deal had been proposed and would probably be accepted, but they were not yet comfortable about it or about
themselves. That discomfort is what I saw around me in their
odd ways of dressing, their fascination with their nerve endings
and taste buds, their distaste for anything mental—which was
the first step toward all that they hated and wanted to escape.

Or maybe I am just old and was feeling old. That would
suffice, would it not, to explain most of my hard feelings?

And what about her? Was she any different from the rest of
them? What was there about her that had attracted me beyond
her beauty and her heartlessness?

Or, perhaps more accurately, why did her beauty and heartlessness distinguish her from the roomful of rather similarly
endowed men and women who were either disturbing or down-
right repellent?

I cannot answer those questions, cannot now and could not
then. And they did occur to me. I remember sitting in a corner
in a club chair upholstered in cream-colored leather and thinking that the manuscript was not all that important. I could
recreate it. I could forget about it, even. But what I could not
do was to endure another hour in this company. I promised
myself that I'd finish my drink and then go.

But Sidonia appeared in the room and managed to throw me
a quick word as she passed on through, "Wait! We'll talk. I
promise."

One more drink, I promised myself. And after that, no
matter what happened, I'd go.

5

WHAT HAPPENED WAS THAT I FELL ASLEEP in that extravagant chair. I remember that I found it interesting to close my eyes and just listen to the phrases that came to the surface as they drifted by. And then there were no more phrases but only Sidonia, touching my earlobe and telling me to wake up. Evidently, I'd made something of a hit. At least I'd been the occasion for somebody's smart remark that, poet or not I was certainly a dreamer, which is almost as good.

"So, you see, I was able to show you off, even if you were being disagreeable."

"Disagreeable? I?"

"You told Feliciana about all those people dying in Africa."

"Surely, she knew that."

"But to remind her of it, to point it out to her . . . As if she could do something to prevent it. As if any of us could!"

"I'm sorry," I said, not wanting to quarrel. Having stayed this long, I wanted my manuscript. At least that.

"Besides, their money comes from Mozambique. Her grandfather was there. Even so, at a party, it isn't nice to have to think of such things."

"I'm sorry," I said again. I managed not to let her guess my satisfaction. It is a gift of dubious value, but it is nonetheless a

137

gift to be the one always to tell the truth—to Salazar, to
Feliciana, and perhaps to Sidonia as well—the unwelcome news
that each of them nonetheless needed. By good luck or bad, I'd
picked out the heiress to that blood money. . . .

"Champagne?" Sidonia offered. "I hadn't meant to bring it
out, but some busybody found it and opened a bottle—which
would be a shame to waste. Shall we share what's left?"

"Of course! To celebrate."

"To celebrate what?"

"The moment. Our being here. Life! Isn't that enough?"

"You should go to work in advertising. For a champagne
distributor."

"If I could find such work, I'd take it in a moment," I told
her.

She handed me a flute of champagne, kicked off her shoes,
sat down in a nearby chair, and without any word of a toast or
even that minimal gesture of the raising of her glass, gulped.

"Tell me about yourself," I suggested. Sometimes that works.

She glared at me. "Now that I have become your muse, you
feel you are entitled to details about my life?"

"Not at all. On the contrary! The more I know about you as
an individual human being, the less I am likely to burden you
with those inspirational duties you are so reluctant to assume. . . ."

"I don't know whether I'm reluctant or not. It's not something I've done before. Or even an ambition I ever had—like
taking flying lessons, for instance."

I shrugged. "If you'd rather not confide in me . . ."

"No, no. I don't mind. But you might not like it. I might not
be able to hold the pose on that mental pedestal you've got me
on, or not with the right authority and conviction."

"Try me," I offered. "At the worst, I can fail you. I don't see
how you can fail me. Muses never fail."

"Perhaps the myth needs to be revised."

"An interesting idea," I said, taking another sip of the wine.
"The liberated muse! A kind of chum. Something between a
coworker and a managing partner."

"I don't know if I like that any better," she said. But she commenced nevertheless to tell me about herself, about her childhood on the family estates, about her series of guerilla battles with her parents and especially with her father, and even about some of her amatory adventures. Her recent excursion to Taormina was especially interesting to me—because I had imagined some such jaunt. I had been incorrect about the details though, settling for Sardinia and a young suitor of whom her father disapproved. The boldness of her choice of a lover who was one of her father's chums and business partners . . . That had been beyond me.

The point of her telling me these things was to see how I'd react, whether I'd be shocked or intrigued or perhaps just disheartened. I knew what to do, though, and took my cue from her. She had been brittle and clever with me; it was the least I owed her in return. I could approve the style of it, surely, but offer a critical suggestion here and there as though I were criticizing the work of a student writer.

What I really felt, of course, was a general distress that a young woman of such gifts, such rare good fortune, should be so unhappy. If she was miserable, what were the chances for an ordinary Portuguese?

"You disapprove?" she asked. It was a challenge really.

"Oh, no. What right have I to disapprove? I'm only sorry you haven't enjoyed yourself more."

She shrugged. "That wasn't the point."

"But it should have been," I said. "To go off for an illicit weekend to a great resort . . . It ought to be enjoyable."

She sighed. "I wasn't the only one there who wasn't experiencing constant delight from morning to night."

"Oh, I dare say. But did that make it any better for you?"

"Not better. Truer."

"Happiness isn't always a fantasy," I told her.

"Isn't it?" she asked. "But it's too late to argue. I'm getting tired. And the champagne is all gone. I'll lend you your manuscript, but will you return it to me? Can I trust you?"

"I trusted you," I told her.

"That was very foolish," she said. "I wouldn't have done that. But then, you were desperate, weren't you?"

"But as you see, I was right," I said.

"It's too late to be clever. Take it. Here it is." She got up and went to the bookcase. From behind one of the rows of books, she produced the brown envelope that held my pages.

"I'm most grateful," I said.

"I think you're crazy," she said.

"Another time, I'll be happy to discuss that with you. Perhaps when I return this. Did you really read it? All of it?" I asked.

"Well, some of it," she said. And then she yawned, covering her mouth with a dainty fist.

I took the hint and my leave.

At any rate, I had it back. But was I better off now or worse? It was not so long ago that this slender sheaf of handwritten pages had been an insurance policy, or at least the frail reed to which I could cling as I tried to keep afloat in the political seas where Salazar and Caetano and Major Pais were the big fish and I was a darting minnow. The PIDE's threats had loomed about me at all times, giving a gravity to the lightness of my duties and a menace to the comfort of my captivity that was so obviously at their pleasure and whim. I remembered having enjoyed the intricate scheming by which I had determined that it was a good thing to have at least one copy outside the palace, where they couldn't lay their hands on it.

Now? I was outside the palace myself, free to walk the streets, to come and go as I pleased, to speak as I liked to anyone who cared to listen—if only I could find such a person. But for how long? I wondered whether, if they were to find this manuscript, they might not at once throw me back into the Aljube?

It is bad enough to learn not to expect rewards and adulation for one's literary productions. But it is hard to accept punishment for having done one's best. That requires more saintliness than I have it in me to imagine, much less attain.

On the other hand, I found myself thinking about Salazar, my master (in the sense of teacher, if not others) and how he had achieved those amazing reversals I'd come to admire. The manuscript that had once been my protection was now, in my possession, under my arm or in a desk drawer, as dangerous as an anarchist's time bomb. One would suppose so, at any rate. Any sudden movement might set it off. But if it were published?

Even if it were in the hands of a publisher? As long as it was under submission, it would fill the function I had in mind for it. If the PIDE were to take me away and stick me in some cell or hide me on some island labor camp, the manuscript would become more valuable. What had been unpublishable before would now become commercially viable. Sensational? Well, not quite, but of a certain timeliness and interest. I would become a martyr and my book would acquire a certain human interest, vulgar perhaps but nonetheless lively.

I figured that if I could work that out, so could some of the people at the PIDE.

The obvious next step was for me to get several copies made so that I could have the book out and under submission at all times. In Lisbon, of course, but in Madrid and Paris and Milan and London, too.

There are lots of publishers. I could keep the ball in play for years, if it came to that.

All that would suffer would be my ego, each time I got another rejection.

Meanwhile, I had a living to make. I needed a job and a place to live, in either order. I went to see an old friend who was an editor at *Epoca,* one of the Lisbon newspapers to which I had occasionally been able to sell my work. As I might have expected, he was not exactly overjoyed to see me. In fact, I had my doubts as to whether he'd be willing to give me even a few minutes of his time. But it would have been most unfriendly, not to say unfair, if I hadn't even shown up in the reception area to try him.

In the event, he had me ushered back to his messy office
with his name and his title—Assistant City Editor—painted on
the door.

"You look well, considering," he said.

"I am well. I've been lucky," I told him.

"So I see. But how lucky? Are you still . . . convalescing?
Are you by any chance still contagious?" he asked, clearly
and yet delicately formulating the question he had as to
whether it would be trouble for him and for the paper if he were
to hire me.

"I believe my recovery is complete. I saw the doctor himself earlier this week, and he seemed to think I was in good
shape."

"The doctor? What doctor?"

"Doctor Pais," I told him.

"You don't say so!"

"Oh, yes. I was at the palace for much of the time, engaged
in sensitive work. . . ."

"I think I'd rather not hear about it, if you don't mind."

"As you like. But there was a conversation I had, just a
few days ago, in which I was told quite clearly that I could
now go about my business. Evidently, I am no longer of
interest."

"Well, that's good to hear," he said.

"But I need work. I'm broke."

"I guessed as much," my friend said. "I suppose we can find
something safe enough. A little dull, perhaps, but if you're
broke, you'll take what you can get, right?"

"Anything!" I said.

"The society page. You can rewrite the engagement and
wedding announcements. You can't get us into a lot of trouble
that way, I shouldn't think."

"I'm deeply grateful. And there will be no trouble, I promise
you."

"I promise you, there will be no trouble," he replied. "We
won't stand for any. You get me?"

"I've got you."

"And I guess we've got you. Start tomorrow?"

"That'd be fine."

"Report to Nuñes. He'll find you a desk."

"Thank you."

He still had twenty hours or so in which to make a telephone call or two and have me checked out, at least confirming that there was no PIDE objection to my working at this absurd and menial job.

I had the rest of the day to find an apartment. Or, more realistically, a room somewhere. Nothing fancy. Not that I'd be able to match my accommodations at the palace, of course, but I'd be free, living my own life.

In this century, a great luxury.

6

FREE, YES, BUT NOT SATISFIED.

To tell the truth, I'd been spoiled. What had changed from my old life? As far as the externals were concerned, very little. But the interiority was different now. I could write what I pleased—on my own time at any rate—and nobody bothered me. I didn't have to worry about Pais, or the PIDE, or Salazar, or all of Portugal.

But that was the trouble. Nobody could bother me because nobody cared, nobody could be distressed or pleased, enlightened or enraged. Nobody hung upon my words, listening intently as Salazar had listened, analyzing my meanings both conscious and unconscious, and seeing through my eyes to a vision of the world reliable enough to trust and act on.

I had no audience.

I came in every morning to the large city room where I had a battered old desk and a reasonably well-maintained typewriter. There was also a telephone by which I could reach some of the people whose information I was to translate into the paper's accepted formulas. Sometimes, I had to ask them questions, the spellings of indecipherable names or even, now and again, substantive information. Is the groom's mother's former husband still alive? Is the bride's address the same as her mother's or has she been living in Lisbon?

Important stuff!

Important to them, at any rate. And if I were to invent even trivial embellishments, putting in an occasional grace note— "balloonist" or "collector of women's footwear"—I could find myself back out on the street in a matter of hours.

These are important people, after all. Not the brides and grooms, perhaps, but their parents, their families. The people whom the editors want to please, and about whom there may even be some curiosity on the part of some of our readers. To suggest that Senhora So-and-so was formerly an aerialist with the Cirque d'Hiver in Paris is an impertinence not to be tolerated either by the lady so described or her family and friends or our readers—not to mention our editors.

But it is tempting. If only to make them pay attention, to insure that they read more closely these boring boilerplate paragraphs.

As long as I stick to the truth, it sticks to me, and I can survive, albeit as the slave of a tyrant more unrelentingly severe than any dictator.

The room I have found is a bare cubicle with a desk, a dresser, a bed, and a chair. Much like my little cubicle in the São Bento Palace. There I had not only a garden to walk in but also the ear of the great man; here I have no garden and am ignored. I can adapt, I suppose. I shall have to learn to adjust.

But it is a great coming down.

Another coming down is my realization that I no longer have such a library to work in (and play in) as I had at the São Bento Palace. I miss the books.

Cut off from the rest of the world, locked away like a monk in one of those grand monasteries we have, the wrecks of which are still imposing . . . but free to follow my whims and hunches, free to do as I liked with much of my time.

Stone walls do not a prison make, etc. But that's nonsense. I was a captive then and I'm free now.

What weighs on me is my inability to use my freedom, to feel comfortable in it, to wear it right.

Verlaine says somewhere that poetry is "inutile." True enough, and even obvious. The cleverness was in the reversal, the way he took something all poets knew and were ashamed of and proclaimed it proudly, even defiantly.

But Verlaine was never a court poet, never had the ear of power, never felt the metaphysical pleasure of creating—not only verses and stanzas but a world to which other men accorded belief, to which other men also subscribed. To which they trusted.

Like Lucretius. Like Dante.

Verlaine was, after all, French. Their important men, their movers and shakers, are the cooks and couturiers upon whom their trade balances depend.

Here, in Portugal, we are explorers. We venture into the unknown and either perish or rule the world.

I had that giddy feeling, I confess, the thrill of making it up as I went along and having others—my shipmates and crew—trust in my hunches.

Out here, in what is politely called the real world, men and women jostle one another in the streets and each of them imagines a whole universe, each of them posits a separate egocentric existence. The national life is a combination of these dreams, a skyscape in which clouds bump into one another in different layers and densities with bolts of lightning occasionally flashing from an upper cloud to a lower, or even, on rare moments, reaching all the way down to earth.

Salazar is packed away like a child's broken toy. And in his absence, one must make do.

As I make do with Sidonia.

How can such a beautiful girl be such a disappointment? What is the point of all that pretty exterior if the inside is shoddy and cheap?

But with whom else am I likely to find even a faint resonance of those remarkable days? Whom else can I expect not just to be interested in my manuscript but changed by it, his or her life fundamentally altered by my words as our world was altered by the writings of Copernicus or Galileo?

She was my Portugal. Or the native queen of the exotic island on which I would found my empire.

She? A dimbulb bimbo like that?

She hadn't even read the book. Just looked at some of it, no doubt sounding out the hard words, syllable by syllable.

What was there ever to lead me to suppose that she even thought about me or my book, that I had penetrated her lovely exterior to reach the sluggish nervous system that had to be buried somewhere within?

I got an invitation to another of her parties! That's what.

I thought of refusing. I hadn't much enjoyed the company at the first party. And I didn't expect to find any friends of hers who would be more congenial. Still, I had nothing else on my calendar for that evening.

Or for that week, if you really want to know.

If I didn't go, I knew I'd hate myself, call myself a coward and a fool. Worse, there would be no more purpose in my manuscript, which would be reduced to the maunderings of a recluse, or the impotent assertion of personality by one who had no particular personality to assert.

The kind of thing Verlaine claimed to find satisfying.

I was also a little worried. I had not intended to screw around at *Epoca,* had resolved to resist the schoolboy temptations that would present themselves often enough. And I had been doing well enough for the most part.

But without my even intending it, in a moment of distracted inattention, I slipped just a little and allowed the word "welder" to intrude itself into the biography of a woman of some social pretension, one of the cosponsors of a tea to benefit a chamber orchestra at the Gulbenkian Foundation.

My editor asked me what I had been drinking the night before and told me to watch myself.

I promised I would do so, but I was worried. If this kind of

thing could be the result of my unconscious mind making its
guerrilla statement, my future at the paper was not secure.

And I realized how much I missed Salazar.

I had promised Sidonia that I would return her copy of my
manuscript. As a man of honor, I owed her at least one more
appearance. Telling myself such things, I persuaded myself that
I had no choice but to accept her kind invitation and, at the
appointed hour—or a quarter of an hour later, to be precise—I
showed up, expecting to find the same brash and cynical group
of privileged brats.

But nobody was there. I thought I might have the evening
wrong. Or that I'd come an hour early.

"No, no. It's the right night. You're on time, or almost," she
told me.

"But where is everyone?"

"It's just you and me. Is that all right? Do you miss the others
so much?"

"No, that's fine," I said, not sure that she wasn't teasing. "I
don't miss the others. Not a bit."

"I thought you wouldn't."

"To what do I owe this good fortune?" I asked cautiously.

"Your muse's whim."

"Ah, yes. That." I'd all but forgotten.

She hadn't forgotten, though. She had decided it was amusing to be a muse, something different, something that couldn't
be bought off the rack in a designer's boutique. The muse of a
real poet. She'd found that collection of verse of mine and
had read it—or so she claimed.

"And the poetry moved you so deeply that you were impelled
to invite me back?" I asked.

She smiled. "Not exactly," she said. "It would be nice if
things happened that way, but . . ." She ended with an airy
wave.

"I didn't suppose so," I said, but I found her candor likable.

"Has your book been published?" she asked.

"These things take time," I told her. "It's under submission."
That was true enough, but I had no real hopes that the book

would do anything—even protect me. I knew that the PIDE could, if they chose, prevent its publication. If they wanted to, they could arrest me, just as before, and find the manuscript, retrieve it from any editor, burn it, threaten him or her . . .

I did not, however, confide any of these gloomy thoughts to Sidonia. Instead, I sat there waiting for her to give me some clue as to how she wanted me to behave. There was some role she expected to play as my muse, and I supposed there would be some corresponding expectations about my role. I didn't want to disappoint her.

"Aren't you going to kiss me?" she asked at last.

That was clear enough. And actually what I had rather expected.

Two cheers for literature!

I did indeed kiss her, delighted with my good fortune, and delighted by how sweet and fresh she was, how she seemed always on the verge of laughter, and how holding her was like holding a brook in my arms so that I could feel its shimmer and babble and play.

We moved to her bedroom where it was obvious that she had expected we would end up. There was an ice bucket with champagne chilling for us. The coverlet was drawn down.

Bliss!

My book, though, had nothing to do with it. Even her fancy that I had chosen her as my muse so that she could perform in the ongoing version of that junior high school pageant she mistook for real life . . . even that had only a tangential relevance. True, poets have been trying for centuries to persuade gullible young women that this is how a muse ought to behave, but Sidonia was mostly immune to these blandishments, having herself very little familiarity with them. There were other more proximate causes of her impulsive generosity.

That friend of her father's with whom she had gone off to Taormina had become something of a pest, was beginning to take her too much for granted, and needed to be taken down a peg or two.

I was the instrumentality for doing that. She would devalue his conquest by bestowing herself on an altogether unprepossessing, pitiable, and almost laughable creature: to wit, myself.

Not quite what I had fantasized. But better than nothing. Better than the alternative about which I asked her at a suitable juncture in the wee hours of the morning. "Why couldn't you simply have lied? Why did you have to do any more than think of the idea? What was there to require you to act it out this way—which is what I really owe my good fortune to?"

Her answer? That she couldn't have been convincing if she had lied. Not just to him, but to herself. It wouldn't have been satisfying just to "make up a story."

Some muse!

7

ON THE OTHER HAND, what is there to complain of? I had been
fortunate beyond my expectations or deserts, having been chosen as the means of Sidonia's rebellion. Without extravagance, I
was in the same boat—if you will pardon the expression—as the
sailors of Os Lusiadas for whom Camões prepares that erotic if
allegorical treat on the Island of Love where beautiful nymphs
weave chaplets of laurel and gold and wreaths of flowers to deck
the brows of their adventurer lovers.

I also had, at last, something in common with the achieve-
ment of my mentor, for if Dr. Salazar could blink the real world
into compliance with his wishes, I had written myself into
Sidonia's bed. I had written my manuscript, sent it to her
for whatever curious reasons, and had followed along after it
with what looked, from a certain vantage point, much like
inevitability.

If she had been a poet, she would not have needed my
collaboration to make good on her claim to her disagreeable
lover or to herself. Had she been an astute reader, she might
perhaps have been able to figure this out.

But I wasn't going to argue. We get what readers we can, and
whether those are the readers we deserve or not is a futile
question.

Imagine Salazar as dictator of Germany. Which is to say, imagine a Hitler who was not anti-Semitic, and who also wasn't crazy or stupid enough to try to fight a war on two fronts simultaneously. Imagine a Germany that did nothing but smash the Soviets and left France and England alone.

On the other hand, imagine a Salazar as the strongman in a country even smaller and less significant than ours. Iceland, maybe.

If Iceland had a dictatorship, more or less restrained, more or less humane, how many years would it take for the rest of the world to notice? And if anyone noticed, who would care?

One learns to work with what is at hand. And to limit one's expectations. Salazar had not tried to regain control of the country but only to exert once more his influence and assert himself on a single question.

To show that he was still alive, still himself, still Salazar.

As a poet, could I be so dense as to disesteem my great triumph? A night in Sidonia's bed and in her arms, and Dante would never have felt the need to write the *Commedia*.

But who is so wise and sane to know these things when the knowledge would do him any good?

My hope was that this would be the first in a long series of nights, each of them as grand or grander, each of them amazing and unforgettable.

The poets know better. A long series of nights like that is a marriage. Which is material not for poets but for novelists.

A single encounter, vivid and wonderful and, because it is never to be repeated, heartbreaking . . . that is poetry. The lyric intensity of the swan song.

And, remember, I had been in prison for months. I had been leading a life of enforced celibacy.

Ah, Sidonia, Sidonia!

Three days later, at my desk at the paper, I was handed an envelope with the lovely de Castro name engraved on its verso. An invitation? A love letter? Ah, my angel!

It was the announcement of Sidonia's engagement. Not to

her father's friend and business associate. And not to me, either.

One of those lunks at the party. The name was vaguely familiar. I could not match it with a face.

But what difference did it make?

In my distress, I found myself thinking about Salazar. He had invited me to return, after all. Anytime.

And good manners dictated that I pay a call on an invalid, express my thanks for what he'd done for me, and ask after his progress.

Maybe he'd even be able to talk a little.

But even his winks and grunts, his sputterings and twitchings that had done so much for me already might offer some further enlightenment or solace or could be of some other unpredictable value.

Or, at the most basic level, Salazar had been lucky for me. Maybe visiting him would be like touching the hump of a hunchback, or giving silver to a gypsy. Or maybe it would just be a lesson in humility and gratitude—that I had not been so afflicted.

There were risks, of course. What if the PIDE decided that I'd gone just a little too far, that I was rubbing their noses in this awkwardness to which I'd been a party?

It is inaccurate to say that I didn't care. Or that I wanted to be imprisoned again. But on the other hand, that was a world I knew and trusted. Keening and complaining were genres I understood.

It is harder to learn to sing paeans and songs of exultation and delight, especially in mid-life, when one has lost the knack for that kind of enthusiasm.

That slight risk of annoying the PIDE only made the visit more attractive, though. If I could defy them, could go and return in safety even there, then there was no reason to doubt the security of the rest of my life.

There was a certain amount of checking back and forth from the gate to some functionary within, who in turn had to clear it

with Dona Maria, but eventually it sank in that I was welcome.
I don't suppose Salazar had a great many visitors at this point.
It would not have been a way to curry favor with the new
regime.

And how many people were likely to show up because they
had a connection that was merely personal, with no political
implications or overtones of any kind?

A dozen? Fewer?

Sad, I decided. But that was the choice he'd made, long ago.

I was ushered down long hallways and up an impressive
staircase with a carved stone balustrade. In the anteroom to the
bedchamber, I waited again while more communications were
exchanged with the inner sanctum. Eventually, I was passed
through.

Dona Maria was pleased to see me.

"You have come to see him," she said. "Good! Unless there
is something you want from him . . . ?"

"No, no. I want nothing. I'm doing fine. But I thought of
him lying in bed and I thought I'd pay a call, just for a
moment. If he's up to it, that is."

"Who knows? He may recognize you. Or not. It is hard to
know anymore."

"He's not doing well?"

She shook her head. "He may have had another stroke. I am
not sure. It is hard to know unless you are a doctor."

"And the doctors won't say?"

"Who can trust them?"

"Let me know when you think I should leave," I told her.

She nodded. And she led me into the bedroom, where the
long table for the cabinet still took up all that space near the
window. The ten chairs of the various ministries were still
arranged in their old places along the sides. The place at the
head, Salazar's place, had always been left empty.

Could he see it? Did it reassure him? Or bother him? Did he
know where he was, or what had happened to him?

I approached the bed and looked down. "Dr. Salazar? How
are you? It is I, Carlos, the poet. Your friend."

He stared up at me.

Or he seemed to be staring. His eyes were open.

"Dr. Salazar?"

Salazar did not blink.

"Can you hear me? Can you still blink?"

Nothing.

"Are you all right? Can I do anything for you? Can I get you anything?"

Nothing at all.

I looked over at Dona Maria. Her face was impassive. No sign of any distress. No tears, certainly. I raised my eyebrows in interrogation, but she made no sign that I was distressing him or that I ought to leave.

I backed off a little and sat down at the closest ministerial chair, which I turned so that I could see him. His eyes had not followed me. He might have been watching a film that was being projected on the ceiling.

"All in favor?" I asked.

"Aye," I answered.

"Opposed?" I asked.

I waited a moment. "The ayes have it, and the motion is carried," I announced.

No reaction. Nothing.

"Is my broadcast booth still there?" I asked.

Dona Maria didn't know what I was talking about. "The booth where I used to broadcast to his radio. I see the radio is still here."

She shrugged. I went to the modified closet where I had once broadcast the news of his imaginary country. Nobody had thought to dissemble the equipment. I turned it on. It still worked. It lit up anyway. I sat down in my old chair and spoke into the microphone. "This is Radio Lisbon! This is the News of the Day!

"In a surprise move today, the Portuguese government declared war on Norway, taking an action the Minister of Disinformation called 'vital to our national interests.' The reason for the declaration was the impossibility of resolving the border dispute that has been the occasion of guerrilla raids on both sides for some years now. When it was pointed out to the

Minister of Disinformation that there is no Portuguese–Norwegian border, he burst into song and produced a bouquet of roses from his ministerial portfolio, which he commenced to eat."

I got up and went back to the bedroom. "Anything?"

Dona Maria shook her head.

I sat down beside the bed. "Are you sure he's alive? He doesn't seem to be breathing."

"He's alive. You can touch him if you like."

I reached out my hand and put it lightly on his chest. He was breathing, slow shallow breaths. He was cool to the touch but not cold. He was alive, but just barely.

"It's as if he's in a trance," I said. "As if he were some Eastern mystic who has managed to withdraw into his own soul."

Dona Maria nodded.

"I owe him," I said. "He got me out of here. It's amazing that he could do anything at all, as sick as he was. But he did. He still had influence, and the courage to use it. Just by blinking. He got me out of here and back into the world. Which was amazing. It all came from here. From you," I said, addressing Salazar now rather than Dona Maria, because it was no more absurd to be talking to him than to her. "That wasn't necessarily your intention. But I'm grateful anyway. You don't mind that, do you?"

No reply.

I shut up. I just sat there for a while, maybe ten minutes, or maybe even twenty. It seemed like a short time that was protracted as in a dream state. Nothing happened. If I concentrated, I could just make out the slightest rise and fall of the coverlet that encased him as he breathed, slowly and intermittently. Now.

And now.

I sat there and watched him breathe.

Then I got up and told Dona Maria that I might return. And that if there was anything she needed, or he needed, if there was anything I could do, she had only to let me know.

She nodded.

8

EAST!

Of course, East. The route to the riches of the Orient. The great exploit of da Gama, our national hero, was to the East where he "obtained by purchase pepper, and mace from the Banda Islands, nutmegs and cloves that were the wealth of the new-found Moluccas, and finally, and as crown of all these, cinnamon, that key to the wealth, fame, and beauty of Ceylon."

I quote from Camões, of course. He was speaking of da Gama, but was it not also the case with Dr. Salazar? Had he too not found his own route to the mysteries and treasures of the East, discovering the secret of their great abnegation, the black hole of their nirvana where even the eternal forms of Plato's abstract universe seem by comparison a welter and clutter? A quiet, an eerie utter silence, a stillness like that of the lotus that floats on the water's surface, a breathlessness as lustrous as any pearl!

To my old nonsense, he had not responded, but that was a perfectly reasonable response. The best response, awesome to behold! Dr. Salazar had attained to a wisdom the sages of the East talk about and that we in the West hardly ever understand well enough even to yearn for.

What is not a dream? There can be no answer to that question—in which case, one does well just to lie there in one's bed where it hardly matters whether the bed is in a grand chamber of a palatial suite or in a corner of some hovel. One dreams what one pleases. Or what one must. Or one does not dream, having been so blessed by the gods as to be excused from any further troubles and vicissitudes.

What he knew, he knew well, and what he loved he possessed.

He had loved Portugal and had possessed her in a kind of bliss I could only imagine with Sidonia. And had he worried about losing her, as any lover must worry about any beloved in this terrestrial existence?

No worries anymore, though. He was now on Camões's Island of Love where the mariners troop ashore in search of fresh meat and sweet water only to realize that they are in a sacred place where there are gods and goddesses and nymphs everywhere. I think it is Lionardo Ribeiro who calls out to Ephyre, one of the nymphs: "You have conquered me, you lovely creature, too lovely to be so cruel. But if you are carrying off my soul, you might as well wait for my body."

Ribeiro runs after her, complaining and beseeching, and she runs away, "not now, as before, to make her pursuivant pay dearly for his prize but in order that she might hear more of his sweet lament and love-lorn complaints. . . ."

And of course she turns and looks at him with tenderness and she laughs and weeps and falls to the ground, and all is forgotten in the ecstasy of love.

And after that?

After that, what could matter? After that, it is enough to lie there in one's bed, stare at the ceiling, and remember. Or not remember.

Perhaps he is still there, at that moment of bliss when he realized that he could make the country do what he wanted, when he understood that his dreams would be acted out by an entire nation of complaisant Ephyres.

Men, women, children, youths and maidens, old dodderers and puling infants by the millions . . .

Ephyres and Sidonias, every one of them! And not in a

remote and imaginary island or in a canto of an old epic, but here, now, in a country in Europe that has postage stamps and an airline and telephone connections to the rest of the world.

And then, suddenly, the route to the East, so sudden and abrupt as to echo Ribeiro's complaint: "If you are carrying off my soul, you might as well wait for the body."

What I saw in the palace was his body waiting patiently for the nymphs to come back and claim it.

Patiently? Say, eagerly.

I was out in the world and I was free. He was still in the palace but he was even more free. He was as free as he had ever been.

I resisted the temptations to describe Sidonia's father as a wrestler and her mother as a lay analyst, or to make the groom's father the abbot of a monastery. I wrote the announcement up the way anyone else would have done it, spelling all the names correctly. Inventing nothing.

It ran in the paper the next day, in the edition that carried on the front page the report that Salazar at last had died.

A relief, as much as an occasion for grief.

His body has gone to join the soul that had already been taken.

He has gone to the front to participate in that war between Portugal and Norway, that bloody battle at our mutual border.

And like Sebastian who still hacks through corpses at Alcácer-Kebir, Salazar may yet return.

For who was seen his body? Oh, yes, we have read of this death in the newspapers, but who believes the papers? Some clown like me could be working at one of these desks in the city room, inventing it all.

Which, considering what runs in the papers, would be rather a relief, wouldn't it?

It takes courage, more courage than I have, to look at things as they are, to see them honestly and not to blink.

Salazarismo!

David Slavitt is the author of many novels, among the most recent of which are *Alice at 80* and *The Hussar*. He has also written several volumes of poetry, including *The Walls of Thebes*, as well as two plays and two works of nonfiction. He has been a film critic for *Newsweek* and has taught and lectured at a number of universities. He currently teaches creative writing at Rutgers University in Camden, New Jersey.